"What made the lumber fall to begin with?" Ken set the mug down and leaned toward Julianna, face intent.

"Well, I–I don't know." How odd it was, that she hadn't even thought of that. She'd been too focused on Ken's safety.

"Neither do I. But I'm going to find out. That lumber didn't accidentally fall just when I was walking by."

Julianna rubbed her forehead. "You're right. Those stacks are perfectly secure. One couldn't collapse unless–"

"Unless somebody made it happen," Ken finished for her, his voice grim.

* * *

Books by Marta Perry

Love Inspired

Love Inspired Suspense

MARTA PERRY

has written everything from Sunday school curriculum to travel articles to magazine stories in twenty years of writing, but she feels she's found her home in the stories she writes for Love Inspired.

Marta lives in rural Pennsylvania, but she and her husband spend part of each year at their second home in South Carolina. When she's not writing, she's probably visiting her children and her beautiful grandchildren, traveling or relaxing with a good book.

Marta loves hearing from readers and she'll write back with a signed bookplate or bookmark. Write to her c/o Steeple Hill Books, 233 Broadway, Suite 1001, New York, NY 10279, e-mail her at marta@martaperry.com, or visit her on the Web at www.martaperry.com.

Marta Perry

In the Enemy's Sights

Steeple
Hill®

Published by Steeple Hill Books™

Special thanks and acknowledgment
are given to Marta Perry for her contribution
to the FAITH AT THE CROSSROADS series.

This story is dedicated to my dear Love Inspired
sisters, with thanks for your love and support.
And, as always, to Brian.

STEEPLE HILL BOOKS

Steeple
Hill®

ISBN 0-373-87359-X

IN THE ENEMY'S SIGHTS

Copyright © 2006 by Harlequin Books S.A.

www.SteepleHill.com

Printed in U.S.A.

The Lord is my light and my salvation; whom should I fear? The Lord is the refuge of my life; of whom then should I be afraid?
—*Psalms* 27:1

CAST OF CHARACTERS

Kenneth Vance—He was shot down while on a mission, but would recovery in Colorado Springs prove even more dangerous for this Air Force pilot?

Julianna Red Feather—This expert in canine search-and-rescue was feeling burnt-out emotionally and spiritually, but her job wasn't over yet....

Jay Nieto—The Native American teen Julianna had taken under her wing was a good assistant during the canine training, but was he also responsible for the vandalism at Montgomery Construction?

Maxwell Vance—Now that the mayor has taken a turn for the better, will the powers that want him dead finally succeed?

ONE

If he stayed inside for another minute, he'd probably explode. Grateful for the phone call that had distracted his friend, Kenneth Vance stepped from the office into the yard of Montgomery Construction Company. Behind the long, low office building loomed the old red barn that had been the original site of the company. Now, eight-foot-high chain-link fencing surrounded a whole complex of buildings.

Beyond the fence, Ken could see a steady flow of traffic on the industrial park road. Colorado Springs seemed to have grown in the years since this place, in the shadow of Pikes Peak, had been home to him.

When he moved beyond the shade of the overhang, the Colorado sunshine, fierce even in April at this altitude, hit him like a blow. He groped for the dark glasses he'd been forced to wear since the incident.

Incident. That was the term the Air Force used. The official verdict had been that his jet was brought down over South America by insurgents armed with a shoulder-fired missile. Somehow *incident* didn't seem a strong enough word for something that ruined a man's life.

He pushed the thoughts away forcefully and wandered farther into the yard. Quinn Montgomery, his longtime friend and owner of Montgomery Construction, had made progress in repairing the destruction done by an arson fire at the yard last month, but a jumble of broken concrete and charred timbers still marred the scene.

Ken stiffened, trying to will away the incessant blurring of his vision that was an annoying leftover from his injuries. Someone was moving around in the debris. No one should be there.

He strode quickly toward the spot. With all the misfortunes that had dogged the Montgomery and Vance families lately, he wasn't taking anything for granted.

"Hey! What are you doing here?" It was the command tone that was ingrained after eight years as an Air Force officer.

Maybe not much longer, a small voice in the back of his mind reminded him.

A slight figure emerged from a fractured piece of concrete pipe. A teenage boy, he thought for an instant, maybe from one of the street gangs Quinn said had begun to appear on the usually placid streets of Colorado Springs in recent months.

Then the figure straightened, and he realized it was no boy. Slim, small, but certainly no boy. The woman had glossy, straight black hair in thick braids. High cheekbones increased the faintly exotic quality of her looks, and dark eyes met his with a startled wariness.

"What did you say?" Her voice was soft, a little husky. Something about it rang a bell, but he couldn't place her.

"I asked what you're doing here."

He took a step toward her and then froze. A dog came out of the pipe behind her—a big German shepherd that lowered its head and growled at him, pressing close to the woman's side.

"Easy, Angel." Her hand caressed the animal's head. "He's a friend."

Something about the way she said the word increased that sense of recognition. He frowned, annoyed that he couldn't remember. "Do we know each other?"

Her glance touched his face and flickered away. "We did. A long time ago. You're Ken Vance." She smiled faintly. "Everyone in The Springs has heard you're back."

True enough, he supposed. When you belonged to the Vance family and your uncle was the mayor, everyone knew too much about you. They probably even knew why he was here, out of uniform, instead of doing what he was born to do.

"You must have changed more than I have." He tried to manage a smile. "I know I know you, but—" Recognition came then. "You're Julianna Red Feather, aren't you?"

"Yes." She met his gaze squarely, without a hint of embarrassment.

"It's been a long time." He probably felt embarrassed enough for both of them, even though he hadn't thought of that awkward incident in years. Still, meeting her again was easier since she'd obviously gotten over that foolish crush she'd once had on him. "You've changed."

She shrugged, a smile lightening her grave expression. "I've grown up. We all have. And, by the way, I do have permission from Quinn to be here."

"Right." Of course she did. He'd been needlessly officious.

Julianna *had* changed. He remembered a girl so shy she'd nearly vanished into the woodwork in high school—one he'd thought had been ashamed of her Native American ancestry. Now she confronted him with confidence, head held high. Her thick braids with their woven ties and the turquoise emblem she wore at her throat seemed to announce pride in her heritage.

"So, you two remember each other, do you?"

He hadn't heard Quinn approach, but there he was, grinning at them. Quinn bent to ruffle Angel's ears, obviously friends with the dog.

"We've figured it out," he said easily, wondering what the relationship was between Quinn and Julianna. He'd been away for years, except for flying visits when he was on leave. Anything could have happened, and he wouldn't necessarily have heard unless his mother had thought to mention it in one of their frequent phone conversations.

"Julianna's the newest member of Montgomery Construction Company," Quinn said, answering the question in his mind. "She's running the office for us now."

He lifted an eyebrow. "You expect your office manager to clean up the scrap yard?"

"Julianna didn't tell you?" Now it was Quinn's turn to raise his brows. "She and Angel are also members of a FEMA Urban Search and Rescue team. She thinks this mess I haven't cleared up yet will be an ideal site for training exercises for her team."

"No, she didn't mention it." He smiled at Julianna, relieved that they'd moved past a rocky beginning. "You've turned into a talented lady."

She shook her head slightly, something guarded in her dark eyes.

"We're proud to have her here." Quinn patted her shoulder, not seeming to notice. "She and Angel have gone to rescue sites all over the place. They're heroes."

"I'm impressed." He didn't know how the dog felt about it, but Julianna was obviously embarrassed. Or was the feeling something deeper than embarrassment? He wasn't sure.

Quinn gave him a challenging look. "You know, buddy, you could do worse than join the team here at Montgomery Construction while you're home on leave. I could use you, and you'd like it here. Wouldn't he, Julianna?"

The proposal startled him, but before he could respond, something else startled him even more—the look in Julianna's face at the comment. Dismay filled her dark eyes before she masked her expression.

"I'm sure he would." She turned, clicking her fingers to the dog. "You'll excuse me, won't you? I need to get back to work."

Woman and dog moved quickly away. He watched Julianna's slim, straight back for a moment before turning a frowning glance on Quinn.

"I'm not looking for charity." His voice grated on the word. "Thanks, anyway."

"Good thing," Quinn replied evenly. "Since I'm not offering it."

"Nice try, Q, but I don't know a thing about the construction business and you know it." He didn't know about anything but flying. And if he couldn't do that—"Did my mother put you up to this? Or Holly?"

It would be just like his twin sister to interfere. She was so eager to distract him from his troubles that she was driving him nuts.

"Nobody put me up to anything," Quinn said. "You always were too stubborn for your own good."

"You're a good one to talk. Your father used to say you could give lessons to a mule."

Once Quinn made up his mind to something, there was no moving him. Maybe that quality in common had helped forge their friendship.

Quinn shrugged. "Face it, buddy. You need something to occupy your time while you're stuck on medical leave, or your loving family will drive you crazy fussing over you."

True enough, but Quinn's job offer still sounded like charity.

"And I need someone I can trust around here." Quinn paused, his usual smile dimming. "You know that we seem to have become a target in the past few months, don't you?"

He nodded. "I've heard something about it. My mother keeps trying to protect me from hearing anything bad, but she couldn't prevent my knowing about the fires. Or about Uncle Max getting shot."

Maxwell Vance had been in a coma since the shooting, a continuing grief to the family. Some people said he'd made too many enemies during his brief term as mayor by taking a hard line on drugs.

"That's been a tough situation. You know we're all praying for him."

"Yes. Thanks." His throat tightened at the thought.

Quinn's face darkened. "As for the fire, the investigators seem to think Neil O'Brien was responsible. You wouldn't know him, probably. He was an assistant fire chief."

"Was?"

"The department suspended him while the investigation's going on. There's even a rumor he may have been involved in drugs."

"You'd think they'd have him under arrest, then."

Quinn shrugged. "Suspicion isn't evidence. On the surface, there's no connection between that and your uncle's shooting and the vandalism we've been having, but I'm not taking any chances."

"I don't know much about security, either."

In fact, he didn't know much about any job, other than flying. Bitterness washed over him. If God were really in control, why were all these bad things happening to them?

"Maybe not, but you're smart and you're tough. And I can trust you." Quinn nudged his shoulder. "Anyway, you owe me. Think of all those times I got slammed to the turf protecting the quarterback so you could throw a touchdown pass."

"If that's how you remember it, maybe you hit the turf a few too many times." He grinned, suddenly feeling a little more like himself again. At least Quinn didn't treat him like an invalid. "All right, sign me up. I'll do it."

Quinn grabbed his hand and shook it, obviously pleased with his decision. Maybe now wasn't the moment to add the reservation in his mind.

I'll do it...for the time being. But when this injury heals, when I can see well enough to fly again, I'll be out of here in a hurry.

He had to say *when*, not *if*. He couldn't handle any other possibility.

Quinn clapped him on the shoulder. "Come inside, and I'll go over the operation with you. We'll tell Julianna to spread the word, so everyone knows why you're poking around."

Julianna. A faint unease entered his mind. Julianna had been dismayed at the prospect of Quinn offering the job. How was she going to react now that he'd accepted it?

Two days had passed, and Julianna still wasn't used to seeing Ken every day. She frowned at her computer screen. It was tough to concentrate when he could walk in the door at any moment.

At least Ken seemed to spend most of his time out in the yard or at the site of the company's biggest project, the new physical therapy wing of Vance Hospital. The ongoing cases of vandalism there had everyone on edge.

So he wasn't here, and even if he were, she'd cope. She wouldn't let herself think about what had happened between them once upon a time.

She stared at the figures on the screen, but they seemed to blur. Instead she saw a high school corridor, lined with lockers. Ken leaned against one, his red letter jacket standing out against the gray metal. She'd known that locker well—she'd certainly spent enough time lurking in the hallway to catch a glimpse of Ken.

She must have been crazy that day. It was the only explanation that made any sense. He'd noticed her, smiled at her, and she'd blurted out her love without a thought for the consequences.

Her face burned even now at the thought of his appalled expression. She'd whirled at the sound of laughter to find several of his buddies behind her. They'd heard. They'd laughed. And it had been all over school in a day.

To give Ken credit, he'd tried to be kind to her after that, but she couldn't accept kindness from him. Since her grandparents wouldn't let her quit school, she'd had to tough it out. She put on the poker face she excelled at, courtesy of the Zuni Pueblo side of her family, and pretended not to hear the whispers and snickers.

Somehow she'd gotten through the rest of that year. Eventually people had found other things to talk about, the excitement of graduation wiping everything else from their minds.

She'd survived. She'd made a success of her life. She wouldn't let a high school mistake affect her job.

They'd both changed. She'd said something like that to Ken, and it was true. The lithe, smiling boy had turned into a strong, broad-shouldered man. The responsibility of command had put lines in his face, emphasizing his maturity, but his golden-brown eyes still seemed to look toward the skies.

Somehow she thought the lines of tension around his lips were recent, the product of the trials of the past few months. The crash had left a few visible scars on him, and probably many more that weren't so visible.

Her heart seemed to wince at the thought. *Be with him, Lord. He's struggling now—I know it.*

She could pray for him, but that was all she could do. Kenneth Vance was out of her league. He had been in high school, and he still was. She tapped the keys, determined to concentrate on the report and banish Ken from her thoughts.

Unfortunately for her concentration, the door banged open. Somehow she knew without turning around that it was Ken. Well, they were colleagues now. She could act like a friend.

"How's it going?" He came to perch on the edge of her desk, looking as if all he had to do all day was sit there and watch her. In jeans and a sweatshirt, he had a casual charm. She could imagine how devastating he'd be in his Air Force uniform.

"Fine." She perched her hands on the keys and tried to look busy. "Are things quiet down at the site?"

"Minor vandalism." He frowned, lines forming between his straight eyebrows. "The cops think it's just resentment from people who were relocated when the hospital took over that block."

"That's natural enough, I guess. No matter how run-down the houses were, they were home to someone."

He rubbed the left side of his forehead, the side

where the puckered scar was dangerously close to his eye. She shuddered a little inside. Holly, Ken's sister, had told her that Ken's vision was affected by the accident—that was why he couldn't fly. Any closer and he'd have lost the eye entirely.

"What?" He was frowning at her now, and she knew she'd stared at him too long.

"Nothing. I was just thinking that you looked as if you have a headache. Maybe you should take a break."

He stood abruptly, his posture straight. Military. He looked at her as if he'd never met her.

"I'm fine. I don't need anyone fussing over me." He wheeled and stalked out.

That went well. She pressed the heels of her hands against her eyes.

Ken didn't want to be her friend. He didn't need anyone else to care about him.

What did she expect? He had hordes of friends and family just waiting to help him. But did they see what she saw? Did they see the scars the accident had left on his soul?

Maybe she recognized it in him because she'd been there, too. She knew what it was like to feel like a failure. To feel that God had deserted you.

Images rocketed through her mind, and she forced them away. She couldn't control the pictures when they came to her in her dreams at night, but she could when she was awake. She wouldn't let them in.

That made it all the more impossible for her to help Ken, even if he'd been willing. She'd just begun trying to stumble her way back to spiritual wholeness. She couldn't help Ken, because she wasn't even sure she could help herself.

The stained-glass windows of the church parlor were dark images at night, but the room was warm with lamplight and the buzz of soft conversation. Julianna had been attending the evening Bible study for only about a month, but already she felt at home here. Pastor Gabriel Dawson had the gift of making everyone who walked through the door feel welcome.

The grandfather clock in the corner of the parlor struck the hour, and at the signal people began finding seats. The older folks settled into the conversational grouping of couches and love seats. Julianna slid into the back row of folding chairs.

She glanced toward the door. Holly Vance, now Holly Montgomery since her marriage, was usually here by this time. Of course, with the excitement of having her brother home, to say nothing of her pregnancy and taking care of her husband and home, she could have decided to skip tonight's session.

The door opened. Holly came in, the aqua sweater she wore laying smoothly over the rounded bulge of her pregnancy.

Julianna smiled, meeting her eyes, and waved. Holly waved back, a little wiggle of her fingers indicating they'd sit together.

And then Julianna saw who came in the door behind her. Ken.

Several other people saw Ken at the same time, and

they began getting up, surrounding him to shake his hand or hug him. Their welcomes gave her the minutes she needed to compose herself.

She should have guessed Holly might bring him. She was Ken's twin, after all, and she was probably the closest to him of all his numerous relatives. Right now Holly was beaming, obviously considering it a coup that she'd succeeded in getting him here. She looked up at her tall brother with such pride and pleasure that it made Julianna blink back tears.

By the time they sat down beside her, she was able to smile, appear composed and act as if it didn't matter in the least that the object of her high school dreams was sitting next to her. But she was thankful when Pastor Gabriel began the study and she could focus her attention on him.

It wasn't the fault of Pastor Gabriel's excellent presentation on Psalms that her gaze strayed to Ken's strong hand, clasped tightly on his knee. Judging by the set to his jaw and the tension in his hand, Holly's plan to bring him tonight wasn't as successful as she might have hoped.

It also wasn't Pastor Gabriel's fault that it was taking all her strength to keep the dark images at bay. Maybe she should blame that on Ken. It was his stress that was fueling hers.

She tried to focus on the psalm they were discussing. "The Lord is my light and my salvation; whom should I fear?" Was that what kept coming between her and God—fear? Fear that she couldn't cut it any longer, that her courage was gone for good, that she'd let someone else die—

Now it was her hands that clasped tightly enough to hurt. And she felt Ken's gaze on her, noticing, probing. Deliberately she relaxed her hands, not looking at him.

Pastor Gabriel asked for prayer requests as he ended the session. Several people mentioned concerns. She pulled out her notebook to jot them down so that she could continue to pray during the week.

Holly, voice lilting, asked for prayers of thanksgiving for Ken's safe return. Then she turned toward Ken, as if inviting him to share a request as well.

He wasn't going to. Julianna knew it and thought it strange that Holly didn't. His bitterness washed over her in a wave, so strong that it almost obliterated Pastor Gabriel's voice, raised in prayer.

When the prayers were over, people pressed around them again—to see Ken and Holly, not her. She picked up her coat and began to edge her way along the row of chairs. But before she could gain freedom, Holly linked her arm with Julianna's, immobilizing her there at her side.

"It's just been so nice to see all of you, but we really have to get going." Holly beamed impartially at everyone. "See you Sunday."

She hooked her other arm with Ken's, leading them toward the door. The three of them stepped out into the cool, misty darkness.

"Rain coming," Ken said, with the authority of one

to whom the weather was an important consideration. "I think the little mother should get home."

"Not yet," Holly said. "Let's go out for coffee. Jake's working late tonight, and I don't want to go home to an empty house."

Somehow Julianna didn't think that was Holly's only reason, but she couldn't find the words to refuse. Holly, chattering enough for all of them, didn't give either of them time to object as she piloted them out the walk to the street.

A few minutes later, the three of them were ensconced in a cozy booth at the coffee shop on the corner. The rain Ken predicted had begun to streak the plate-glass window, and the place was empty except for them and an absorbed-in-each-other couple in the back booth.

Holly beamed at them once they'd ordered their coffee. "This is so nice—going out with two of my favorite people."

Ken eyed her warily. "I'm glad you're happy, Hol. But you didn't need to finagle me into going to Bible study in order to spend some time with me."

"I didn't. I'm just so thankful you're still with us that I have to praise God for it about every minute-and-a-half." Tears made her eyes brilliant. "You can't blame me for that, can you?"

"I guess not." Ken frowned. "But you know, Holly—"

Holly glanced at her watch. "Oh my goodness, I didn't realize how late it was. I've got to get home." She slid out of the booth before they could react. She divided her smile between them. "You stay, have coffee, talk. We'll get together again soon."

She whirled, her jacket flaring, and hurried out.

For a moment Julianna couldn't speak. What was Holly thinking? Ken stared after his sister, a bemused expression on his face. Finally he shrugged, smiling a little.

"I'm sorry."

She blinked. "For what?"

"My sister, the matchmaker." He shook his head. "She can't seem to help it. She's happily married, she's having a baby and she's busy trying to match everyone else up in pairs, too."

"The Noah's Ark syndrome," Julianna suggested.

"Something like that." He sobered. "She doesn't realize—" He stopped, and she couldn't guess what he was thinking. "Well, that everyone isn't ready for that."

"I guess not." She stared down at the coffee she was stirring, not wanting to look at him.

"I hope it didn't embarrass you."

She forced herself to meet his gaze. "Of course not. Why would it?"

His brown eyes were filled with nothing but kindness. "After what happened between us back when we were in high school, I thought it might. I'm sure Holly didn't think about that."

She managed a smile. "She didn't, and I didn't either. It was a long time ago." *Liar*, her mind whispered to her. *You've been thinking of it too often since Ken's return.*

"That doesn't mean I shouldn't apologize for acting like a jerk."

"I barely remember it, but I'm sure you didn't do anything of the kind." *Please, don't let him read anything in my voice.* "Just forget it."

"Okay." He spread his hands, as if to show they were empty. Strong hands, with a barely healed scar across the back of the right one. "It's gone. Tell me about you. I want to hear all about this search-and-rescue work of yours."

"There's nothing to tell." Ken seemed determined to bring up every painful subject he could tonight. "Angel and I have been working together for several years. She's really the hero, not me."

"Quinn said you'd worked all over the place."

"That might be a slight exaggeration. We go wherever FEMA sends us. Usually we don't stay more than ten days at a time on a job—after all, we're all volunteers."

"Must be a tough ten days, going to where there's such devastation."

"Yes." The word came out short, because the images were drawing closer. "What about you? You must have had some exciting adventures in the military."

She knew it was the wrong thing to say as soon as the words were out of her mouth, but she'd been desperate to turn the conversation away from her own pain. His face tightened, and he stared down at the scarred tabletop.

"Some."

Silence stretched between them, colored with pain. Frustration. Bitterness.

Poor Holly. She thought she was doing a good thing, trying to bring her friend and her brother together. She didn't realize the truth.

The truth was that she and Ken were both fighting something that could very well beat them. She didn't know what it was for Ken, except that it had something to do with his crash. She knew what it was for her, but she didn't know what to do about it.

That was what Holly didn't understand. Neither she nor Ken was ready for matchmaking. She didn't know about him, but maybe she never would be.

TWO

"Okay, come on. One more time." Julianna gave an encouraging smile to the new volunteer who was trying to master searching the debris field. They'd stayed on after the team drill for some private practice.

"It's no good." The young woman shook her head, wiping her face with a muddy hand. "I can't get Queenie to cooperate."

"Queenie's doing fine." Julianna patted the golden retriever's head. "She's depending on you for direction, Lisa. You just have to make it clear what you want. One more time, and then we'll quit for the day."

Jay Nieto, leaning against a pile of lumber, sighed elaborately, and Julianna shot him a reproving look. She was paying the teenager to assist her with the drill not because she needed help, but because Jay, like so many young teens, needed something to keep him off the streets.

"Okay." Lisa straightened. "One more time."

Jay, who'd been playing the role of victim, criss-crossed the muddy lot, moving between and over the debris piles. Then he ducked inside one of the concrete pipes and pulled a piece of plywood over the entrance.

Lisa waited a moment, watching Julianna. At her nod, she gave the order to Queenie. The two of them started across the field, Queenie's plumy tail waving.

"Are they having problems?" Ken spoke for the first time, but she'd been aware of him, standing and watching, for the past hour.

Too aware. It had made her jittery, that steady gaze, and maybe the dogs had picked up on her feelings.

"Not really. Lisa's a fairly recent volunteer, so she and Queenie don't have much search experience. But they'll work it out."

She nodded, satisfied, as Queenie lifted her head and sniffed, then gave a soft woof.

"There, she's got it now. Search-and-rescue dogs have to be able to pick up the scent from the air."

"Angel looks as if she's thinking she could do it better." He bent to pat her dog.

"Angel always thinks that." The dog looked up at the sound of her name, tail wagging.

Queenie had reached the pipe now. She pawed at the board Jay had pulled across the entrance, barking furiously. Lisa joined them and the two of them "discovered" Jay, who climbed out with a bored look.

"Good job, Lisa," Julianna called. "Reward her now."

Lisa, hugging Queenie, responded with a brilliant smile.

"You were right to push her to try once more," Ken observed. "You never want to end a training session on a failure if you can help it."

"I try. Sometimes it's a tough call, but I knew they could do it if they just got out of each other's way. They have a long way to go, but they have the right stuff."

His smile flickered. "I usually hear that expression about pilots, but I guess it applies. How long will their training take?"

"Two years, if Lisa wants FEMA certification. I'm pushing her to do that. We don't have nearly enough trained teams available."

He whistled softly. "I had no idea there was so much to it. If it's volunteer work, who pays?"

"The volunteer." That was what most people didn't understand. "Hours and hours and hours of work, and plenty of money for materials. We're only paid when we're actually deployed."

"You have to be dedicated, don't you?"

She thought she detected admiration in the glance he sent her way and hoped she wasn't blushing. "We're always scrambling to find places to train that won't cost us. That's why it's so good of Quinn to let us train here."

"Well, the Montgomerys and Vances owe you. We learned firsthand the value of what you do when you found my brother and his girlfriend in that mine collapse at the ranch."

She ducked her head at the implied compliment. At least they were talking easily to each other now. After the way things had gone at the coffee shop a few nights ago, it was more than she'd hoped for.

Lisa came up to her then, and she was distracted from Ken's presence for a few minutes while she gave the young woman some suggestions for their next practice. When she turned back, she found Jay Nieto looking up at Ken with something akin to worship in his eyes.

"Did you two introduce yourselves?" she asked.

"Are you kidding?" Jay had lost the bored expression that was becoming habitual. "I know who he is. Major Kenneth Vance. He's an Air Force pilot."

The aliveness in Jay's eyes startled her. It was the most interest he'd displayed in anything other than the gang of older kids he kept trying to impress.

That gang and their leader, Theo Crale, was the main reason she'd taken an interest in the boy. If she could keep Jay out of a street gang and keep him in school, he might have a decent future. Given Jay's unexpected enthusiasm, Ken's presence could be an incentive to keep Jay interested in working for her.

"That's right," she said. "He's helping out here while he's home on leave. Ken, this is Jay Nieto. He's been giving me a hand with the training."

"Nice to meet you, Jay." Ken held out his hand and Jay took it, color deepening in his thin cheeks.

"You graduated from the Air Force Academy, didn't you? There was a piece in the paper about you when—" He stopped, obviously embarrassed at having made reference to Ken being shot down.

"That's right." Ken's smile was a bit strained, but probably Jay didn't notice. "Are you interested in going to the Academy, Jay?"

Jay's face turned wooden, and he shrugged, his gaze dropping to his sneakers.

She knew that look. She should. It was one she'd worn often enough when she was a teenager, afraid to reach for what she wanted.

"Jay, it's okay to dream big," she said gently.

He shrugged again. "School's for wimps, that's what Theo says."

"Theo's wrong." She wanted so much to make him believe that. "Doing well in school opens doors for you."

"Maybe I don't want doors open." Jay flung his head back defiantly, jet-black hair falling in his eyes. "Maybe I'd rather do things my way, not yours."

"Jay—"

But he swung around and darted off, not even waiting to finish the cleanup work and be paid.

Ken looked after him with raised eyebrows. "Tough guy."

"He'd like to make you think so." She wondered how much to say to him. If she opened up a bit, maybe he'd be willing to take an interest in the boy. "My grandfather knew Jay's family when he lived in New Mexico. Jay is Zuni, like us. When his mother died, his dad moved here, but Jay's had a tough time adjusting to life away from the Pueblo."

"So you're trying to help him."

She shrugged. "I remember what it feels like—not belonging. Unfortunately, Jay's trying to impress the wrong people."

"That Theo he mentioned?"

"He won't get anything but trouble emulating somebody like Theo Crale." She gave him a challenging look. "Now, if he had someone else to look up to, someone he admires—"

Ken's expression turned bleak, his brown eyes seeming to darken. "Not me," he said harshly. "He admires someone who can fly. And that's something I may never do again."

The only light in the abandoned tunnel came from a battery lantern on the rickety table, and the woman picked her way across the littered tunnel floor carefully. She wasn't about to ruin a new pair of Italian shoes just because he had summoned her.

Most people had heard rumors of the tunnels that had once run from The Springs to what had then been Colorado City, the rowdy, wide-open town in frontier days. Colorado City had long since been absorbed into Colorado Springs proper, and the tunnels forgotten, until he had found a use for them. That was like him, to take something and pervert its ordinary purpose to something bent.

She stopped at the table. He'd have heard her come down—he had ears like a fox.

"Stop playing games and come out here. I don't have much time."

A footstep grated, and he appeared in the archway. "You always have time for me, don't you, *querida?*"

She forced a smile, trying to show an affection she didn't feel. "You sound even hoarser than usual. These tunnels aren't good for your throat."

"Yet another thing for which I have to thank the Vances and Montgomerys. Making me hide like a rat in these tunnels, while they live the high life." He yanked out a chair and slumped into it. "I understand Kenneth Vance is back in town."

"So I've heard." She said the words cautiously, not wanting to stir his icy rage to life. He'd been livid at the failure of the attack he'd engineered on Vance's plane through his drug contacts in South America.

"These Vances have more lives than a cat. Just like my new name." He gave a bark of gravelly laughter. "Funny, isn't it?"

"If you say so." She shifted position, careful not to touch the dusty table. "You have something you want me to take care of?"

"Yes." He slapped his palms down on the tabletop. "Kenneth Vance is about to discover that Colorado Springs is just as dangerous as his missions over South America. And since he's spending so much time there, it will be a pleasure to bring Montgomery Construction down with him."

She knew better than to argue, or to wonder how he knew so much about what Kenneth Vance was doing. He had his methods, and he didn't tolerate disagreement with his plans.

"What do you want me to do?"

"Step up the vandalism—not enough to make the police take notice, just enough to make them nervous. I don't want a full-scale investigation at this point. You can use that fool O'Brien."

"He's getting scared. The police are paying too much attention to him."

He glared at her. "He'll do as I say if he knows what's good for him. So will you."

She shrugged. "Of course. Don't I always? I just don't see the point of breaking windows and painting on walls."

"I told you. Make them nervous. Make them wonder. And then, just when the Montgomerys and Vances think success is within their grasp—" He slammed his palm down on the tabletop again, so hard it shuddered. "Then we finish them."

"When did you find this?" Ken barked the question at the night watchman.

Frank Collins bent, his belly straining over his belt buckle as he planted hands on his knees and stared at the slashed tires on the truck. "I told you. Around six this morning."

"Why didn't you call anyone then?"

The man shrugged. "I didn't figure there was anything you could do about it then. I might as well wait until you got here."

"That's not your decision to make. You should have reported." He gritted his teeth. It probably would have done no good, but he still wished the man had followed orders. "Did you find any sign of how they got in?"

Collins shot him a resentful glance. "Nah. Could have come over the fence, I guess."

He suspected Collins hadn't bothered to look. The first thing he was going to recommend to Quinn was that they hire someone else to take over the night patrol. Since that was Quinn's car coming toward them, he wouldn't have to wait long to tell him.

The car shrieked to a stop next to them. Quinn got out quickly, face tight with worry.

Ken glanced at the mechanic who'd been checking the rest of the machinery in the equipment yard. "Jess, did you find anything else?"

"Amateur hour," the man said. "Sugar in a couple of tanks, but we caught it before any harm was done."

Quinn reached them in time to hear that. He ran a hand through his hair, some of the strain leaving his eyes. "That's good to hear. Double-check everything before any equipment goes out of the yard."

"That's going to put us behind at the hospital site," Jess warned.

"Do it as fast as you can, but don't skip anything. I don't want any foul-ups." Quinn turned on Collins. "How could anyone get in here without you spotting them?"

Collins shrugged, not meeting their eyes. "Can't be everywhere at once, can I?"

Quinn made a dismissive gesture. "All right. You can go home."

He waited until the man was out of earshot before snorting. "He was probably asleep in the office the whole time."

"Replacing him is the first thing I was going to suggest," Ken said. "How serious is it to fall behind at the hospital site?"

"Serious." Quinn's face grew tauter. "There's been nothing but trouble there, and the hospital board is looking over my shoulder the whole time. There's a substantial penalty for not completing on schedule. After the losses from the fire, we can't afford to lose anything else."

"I'm sorry, man. You counted on me."

Quinn's expression eased, and he punched his arm. "Forget it. Nobody expected you to spend your nights here. How do you think they got in?"

"Good question." The thoughts that had been lurking under the surface came out. "No obvious break-in signs. I can't help but wonder about the people Julianna had in here yesterday."

Quinn gave a short nod. "Hard to believe, but you'd better check it out. Talk to her."

Easy to say. Not so easy to do. He glanced at his watch. She should be here by now. He'd better get it over with.

Julianna moved away from the window when she saw Ken coming toward the office. It was hard to concentrate on work when everyone had heard about the vandalism, but standing around watching certainly wouldn't help matters.

"How bad is it?" she asked as he came through the door.

"Not as bad as it could have been, I guess." Concern set vertical crease lines between his eyebrows. "Sugar in the gas tanks, some slashed tires."

Ken shrugged out of the denim jacket he'd worn against the early morning chill. Did he realize that the caramel color of the sweater he wore brought out gold flecks in his brown eyes? Probably not, and probably she shouldn't be noticing that.

"Sounds like something teenagers would do."

He nodded, coming to sit on the corner of her desk. "That's what I thought, too. If someone really wanted to cause trouble for the company, they wouldn't bother with such small stuff."

"The police—"

He shook his head. "Quinn doesn't want the police called. The company doesn't need any more negative publicity to make clients nervous about hiring us."

"I understand that, but surely we have to do something—at least try to find out who did it."

"He seems to think I can do that." Ken's frown deepened. "I keep telling him I don't know anything about security, but he won't listen."

"He's known you a long time. He has confidence in you." Odd, that she was reassuring Ken. She'd always thought he had more confidence in himself than anyone she knew. The accident must have dented that somewhat.

"Well, I'm trying." He frowned down at her, and something inside her tightened at his grim expression. "How well do you know the people who were here yesterday for your practice drill?"

For a moment she was speechless. So that was the reason for this little conversation. He wasn't confiding in her. He was questioning her.

She straightened. "How well? Very well. They're people I've worked with for several years, for the most part. They're the kind of people who volunteer their time to do a dirty, dangerous job because they care." She was getting heated, but she didn't care.

"Look, I realize you feel you know them, but—"

She couldn't sit still and listen. She thrust her chair back, standing so that their eyes were level.

"I do know them. They risk their lives for something

they believe in. People like that don't go out and commit vandalism for a hobby." How could he begin to think that?

His gaze was steady on hers. "We don't always know people as well as we think we do."

"I know them." She saw them in her mind's eye. "I trust my life to them when we go out on assignment together. Believe me, I know them."

"What about Jay? Do you know him, too?"

It was as if a pit had opened under her feet, and she teetered on the edge. "I—"

She stopped. She couldn't lie to Ken about the boy, even though she thought she understood him. "I told you. My grandfather has known his family for years. I've known Jay for about five or six months, since he moved here."

"You said he ran with a gang."

Her hands tightened into fists. "I did not say that. He's not a gang member. He's a good kid, a bright kid. He's just looking for a place where he can belong." She looked steadily at Ken. "I know how that feels. That's why I'm trying to help him."

"I'd like to trust your judgment on him, Julianna. But you have to admit, it raises questions. He was here at the yard yesterday, and you told me he's been influenced by some undesirables. And you said yourself the vandalism sounded like something teenagers would have done."

"Not Jay," she said stubbornly, her heart sinking. "Look, if you accuse him of this, you're going to ruin any chance I have of getting through to him."

"If he vandalized your workplace, I'd say you've already lost him."

She wanted to shake him, and she gripped her hands together to keep from giving in to the temptation.

"That's so easy for you to say. You've never had to struggle to belong. You don't have the faintest idea what it's like to be someone like Jay Nieto."

He straightened, his face tightening, giving back glare for glare. "Or Julianna Red Feather?"

"I know who I am." If she were any angrier, she'd strike sparks. "I don't need validation from anyone else."

"Am I interrupting?" The lilting feminine voice from the doorway had both of them swinging around. "I certainly don't want to, but I did think the construction company was open for business." Dahlia Sainsbury lifted a perfectly arched dark eyebrow, looking at Ken as if he were a tall drink and she was thirsty. "Or was I wrong?"

THREE

Ken wasn't sure who disconcerted him more, Julianna with her tacit accusation of prejudice or this woman, with a look that suggested enjoyment at their embarrassment.

Julianna recovered quickly, anger smoothing from her face as if it had never been. "Ms. Sainsbury. I don't believe Mr. Montgomery is expecting you this morning, is he?"

So this woman was apparently a client. Her elegant suit and high heels seemed out of place at the construction company. She let the door click closed behind her.

"I'm sure he'll spare a few minutes to see me. I'd like to discuss the display areas he's designing for the museum. Just let him know I'm here, dear."

There was a casual dismissal of Julianna in her tone. Enough to make Julianna bristle, he'd think, but somehow he was sure that she had already been annoyed from the moment she saw the woman.

Julianna smiled faintly. "I'm afraid Mr. Montgomery is not in the office just now."

"Find him, then," the woman said, her tone dismissive. Without sparing a sideways glance for Julianna, she advanced toward Ken, holding out her hand.

"We haven't met. I'm Dahlia Sainsbury. I'm the new curator of the Impressionist Museum."

He took her hand, aware of the delicate touch of expensive perfume in his nostrils. Everything about Ms. Sainsbury looked expensive, from the top of her sleek, dark head to the gloss of her leather heels. Being the curator of a museum must pay a lot better than he'd have thought.

"Nice to meet you. I'm Kenneth Vance."

She held his hand a little too long. "Of course. Our very own Air Force hero. Naturally I've heard of you."

"Thanks," he said shortly, attempting to draw his hand away.

She put her other hand over his, the gesture implying an intimacy that didn't exist. "It's such a pleasure to meet you. We must get better acquainted. I know several members of your family already. And, of course, Quinn Montgomery."

Julianna didn't seem to be making an effort to find Quinn. "Ms. Sainsbury has asked our cabinetry department to create some display areas for the museum."

The woman's eyebrows lifted. "A job I can find someone else to do, if Montgomery Construction can't handle it."

"I'm sure we can," he said smoothly, not having the faintest idea whether Quinn would agree, but not wanting a potential customer to walk out the door. What on earth was wrong with Julianna? "I think Quinn is out in the yard. I'll just see if I can find him."

Dahlia's smile was triangular, like a cat's. "Send the secretary. You and I can get better acquainted."

Even if he'd been interested, he wouldn't have cared for so blatant an approach. "I'll get Quinn—"

"I'm here," Quinn announced, coming in. "Ms. Sainsbury. How nice to see you. Surely I haven't forgotten an appointment with you, have I?"

Ken stepped back with a sense of relief. Quinn could handle this—he was out of his depth.

"I had some wonderful new ideas for the display area." The woman shifted that intense look to Quinn. "I simply must bounce them off you. I was just telling your girl that I was sure you'd want to see me."

Quinn's smile tightened a fraction at the condescending reference to Julianna, but he took the woman's arm and turned her toward his office.

"I have a few minutes. Let's get your thoughts down." He ushered her into the private office and closed the door.

Julianna tossed the pencil she'd been holding across the desk. It bounced and hit the floor.

Ken picked it up and handed it back. "I gather you don't care much for Ms. Sainsbury."

"I suppose you think she's gorgeous." Juliana bit off the words as if they didn't taste good. "Half the men in Colorado Springs have developed an interest in art since she took over the museum."

He shrugged. "Frankly, I prefer something a little less obvious. Are she and Quinn an item?"

"I hope not." Consternation dawned in her eyes. "I really hope not. But she does seem to be showing up a lot to discuss this project."

"Quinn's a big boy. He can take care of himself." Did Julianna have a personal reason for her concern? "Is there something I should know about between you and Quinn?"

She seemed to forget her annoyance with him in her surprise. "Quinn? No, of course not. We're friends, that's all."

He wasn't sure why that should make him feel relieved, but it did. "Well, whatever she thinks, I'd say his interest in Ms. Sainsbury is strictly business. The company can't afford to lose any jobs, from what I understand."

"True enough. I shouldn't let her get to me that way, but if she calls me 'girl' one more time, I might knock her off her high heels."

"Wait till we've finished her project," he suggested.

That earned him one of those rare smiles that lit Julianna's face and made her eyes sparkle. He'd like to see that expression more often, but it hardly seemed likely.

He leaned against her desk. "Look, about what we were saying earlier. Please believe me. I don't suspect Jay because he's Native American."

"Pueblo," she said. "He's Zuni Pueblo. Like me."

"Pueblo," he agreed. "Wasn't your father—"

"My father was Anglo," she said evenly. "I never knew him. He left before I was born. I barely remember my mother. My grandparents raised me after her death."

Add that to the list of things he'd never bothered to learn about the shy girl who'd sat in front of him in senior English. "I'm sorry. That must have been rough."

"Not at all. My grandparents were wonderful. Still are, in fact."

She'd mentioned that her grandfather knew Jay's family, he remembered. It was a link that probably made her unwilling to think anything bad about the boy.

"In any event, I'm not suspicious of Jay because of his ancestry. Just because he was here, and because of what you said about his connection to a street gang."

She frowned, but at least she wasn't reacting with anger. "I can see why you might think that. All I can say is that I know Jay, and I don't believe he'd do anything that would hurt me. Surely he'd realize I'd be affected by vandalism where I work."

"Teenage boys sometimes don't think with their heads." He grinned. "Believe me, I have vivid memories of the stupid things Quinn and I did at that age. Luckily our parents never found out about most of them."

She smiled in response, but he could still read the concern in her eyes. "Just…be careful of what you say to Jay. He admires you."

That admiration put a sour taste in his mouth, but somehow he'd have to deal with it.

"Look, I'll be tactful, I promise."

He put his hand over hers where it lay on the desk. A sensation of warmth spread up his arm, taking him by surprise, and for an instant he forgot what he was saying.

Then he straightened. "I'll be tactful," he repeated. "But I've got to get to the bottom of this vandalism. Quinn's counting on me. I can't let him down."

She was late for work, Julianna realized as she pulled into her parking space on the gravel lot in front of the office the next morning. She'd had coffee, but still her mind felt fogged, as if the bad dreams that had plagued her all night long were affecting her ability to concentrate.

Well, maybe another cup of coffee would clear her head. She grabbed her bag and hurried toward the office. With any luck, no one else would be here to see her late arrival. Quinn often stopped at one of the job sites before coming to the office, and Ken—

Ken was already here, and he wasn't alone. She stopped just inside the door, her throat tightening. Her grandfather and Ken between them seemed to fill the room—both big men, each with his own aura of power and strength.

Harvey Red Feather sat on the edge of her desk, while Ken leaned against the file cabinet. They each held a coffee mug, and they seemed to be chatting like old friends.

"Good morning, Grandfather. What are you doing here?"

She glanced from him to Ken, realizing that she was the only thing they had in common to talk about. What did Ken think of her grandfather, with his shoulder-length white hair and his serene, weathered face that seemed to have seen and accepted all the world had to offer?

Grandfather got up, smiling, and put his arm around her shoulders. "It's good to see you, little one. I'm a delivery boy. Your grandmother sent lunch over for you. She thinks you don't eat enough." He nodded toward the basket that sat on her desk.

"Some traditional Pueblo dish?" Ken asked.

Grandfather chuckled. "Only if you're from an Italian pueblo. It's gnocchi. Grandma's experimenting with her new Italian cookbook."

"It'll be delicious, whatever it is." She couldn't resist leaning against him. His solid strength reassured her, as it had as far back as her memory went. "But she shouldn't have sent you clear over here just to bring me lunch."

"What do I have to do that's more important than seeing you?" He hugged her. "Besides, I hadn't seen your new workplace yet. Kenneth offered me coffee, so we've been shooting the breeze while I waited for you."

"I'm sorry I'm late." She darted a sideways glance at Ken. He wasn't her boss, but she disliked appearing less than competent in front of him.

He shrugged. "Only five minutes." His gaze seemed to search her face. "You look tired. Maybe you should have taken a few more minutes."

"I'm fine." She evaded his gaze.

Grandfather tilted her chin up, and she couldn't evade his wise, observant eyes. "You do look tired, Juli. Bad dreams again?"

"It's nothing."

She used putting her bag on her desk as a reason to turn away from him. This was why she didn't want the two sides of her life touching. Ken, of all people, didn't need to know about the dreams.

Her grandfather opened his mouth as if to pursue the subject, but Ken broke in first.

"Your grandfather was telling me about the pow-wow that's coming up soon. I didn't know about the

Native American dance competitions. That must be something to see."

He was talking at random, she suspected, trying to edge her grandfather away from a subject that he could see embarrassed her. She hadn't expected such sensitivity on his part.

The least she could do was help skim over the moment. "Grandfather's one of the best dancers. You'd think he was twenty when he gets into the arena. He puts the youngsters to shame."

"Flatterer." Her grandfather hugged her again. "I'd best get home, or your grandmother will wonder what I'm up to. Enjoy your lunch."

"I will. Thank Grandma for me."

He nodded and held out his hand to Ken. "It was a pleasure to meet you. If you'd like to visit the powwow, you'd be more than welcome. Get Juli to bring you."

"Thank you, sir. I just might do that."

Her grandfather went out, letting in a wave of cool morning air that cooled her warm cheeks. Once the door closed behind him, she glanced at Ken.

"It was nice of you to express an interest, but you don't really need to attend the powwow. I don't think it would be something you'd care for."

"What makes you so sure?" He came to perch on the corner of her desk where her grandfather had sat. Unfortunately the feeling she had when he was that close was entirely different. "Sounds pretty interesting to me."

She shrugged. "It's mainly for Native Americans."

"Your grandfather said I'd be welcome."

Why was he so persistent about something that couldn't possibly interest him?

"You'd be welcome," she said shortly. "I just don't think you'd enjoy it."

"Is it that you don't want to take me?" He leaned toward her across the desk. "Or are you ashamed of your heritage?"

Her head came up at that. Maybe she'd felt that way once, when she'd been a shy teenager desperate to fit into an Anglo world, but no longer. "I'm proud of who I am."

"It's me, then, is it?"

"No." He was pushing her into a corner, and she didn't appreciate it. "If you'd like to go, I'd be happy to take you." She flashed him an annoyed look. "Satisfied?"

His lips twitched. "Pretty much. It's a date."

No, it wasn't. But if she said any more about it, he'd think she attached too much importance to the whole idea of going somewhere with him.

She switched on her computer and opened her e-mail, hoping Ken would take the hint. He didn't move.

"Your grandfather was right. You do look tired. Want some coffee?"

"I can get it—" she began, but he was already crossing to the coffee pot.

"I've got it. Hope you can drink my brew. I needed something to keep me awake."

She took the mug he handed her. Now that she looked, she saw the marks of sleeplessness on his face that must also be evident on hers. Was Ken troubled by dreams, too—dreams of his plane spiraling toward the earth?

"What kept you up?" She sipped at the hot, strong coffee, and it nearly scalded her mouth.

"The new man Quinn hired for the night patrol couldn't start for a couple of days, so we took turns doing some random checks overnight." He ran his hand through his short brown hair. "Guess I've gotten out of the habit of working odd hours."

"I didn't realize." Her thoughts darted to Jay. "Was everything quiet?"

His face tightened. "Quiet enough here. But while we were putting extra protection here, vandals went after the hospital site."

"Oh, no." They both knew the company couldn't stand any more delays on the project.

"Quinn's down there now, trying to get things moving again." He shook his head, the lines etching deeper on his face. "I don't know what's going on, Juli. But I've got a bad feeling about it."

"This vandalism has everyone jittery," Julianna said, pulling back into her parking spot at the office that night. Angel, sitting beside her, gave a soft woof, as if to express interest.

"And it's a good thing I have you to talk to, or I might start talking to myself." She rubbed behind Angel's ears, earning a rough, wet kiss from the dog's tongue. "Come on, girl. I just need to pick up Gram's basket, and then we'll go home and have a run before bed."

Maybe a good long run would tire her out enough to sleep tonight without dreams. One thing about having

Angel along—she could run any time of the day or night without fearing for her safety. Nobody messed with a woman accompanied by a German shepherd.

The office was dark and quiet. She picked up the basket she'd left on the counter next to the coffeemaker. No one would appreciate coming in to leftover gnocchi congealing in the casserole dish. Good as it had been, she hadn't been able to finish it. She'd intended to have the rest for supper, but she'd gotten busy and forgotten to take it home.

Well, everything seemed quiet enough tonight. She went out, Angel at her heels, and locked the door behind her. As she set the basket on the backseat of the car, Angel woofed softly. She glanced at her.

The dog stared into the shadowy yard, her ears pricked up, tail waving.

"What is it, girl?" She closed the car door, looking across the yard, her eyes adjusting to the dimness. "Do you see someone?"

No. Angel had heard something, and now she heard it, too—a soft footfall, somewhere beyond the circle of light cast by the fixture over the office door.

A frisson of apprehension slid across her skin. It was probably nothing—just the night watchman on his rounds. But with everything that had happened lately, she couldn't ignore it.

Making a swift decision, she took the flashlight from the glove compartment and locked the door. She dropped the key into the pocket of her jean jacket and turned toward the yard.

Angel was with her. She didn't have to fear any intruder—one snarl from the dog would probably be enough to send anyone running.

She started toward what she thought was the source of the sound, moving quietly, Angel close against her side. She strained her ears for any noise, even knowing that Angel would hear anything first.

Pallets of lumber, arranged in rows, innocent enough in the daylight, loomed over her like pallid giants, waiting to pounce. There were too many hiding places in the dark. She sent the beam of her flashlight probing along the row, lighting up the dark corners.

Nothing. Maybe she'd imagined the sound. Or it was the night watchman moving along on his lawful rounds.

But that rational explanation didn't erase the apprehension that skittered along her skin, making the hair stand up on her arms.

Angel's hair stood up, too, making a ruff around her neck. Because the dog picked up on her nervousness, or because Angel sensed something wrong, too? Impossible to tell, but dog or human, the response was the same.

They reached the end of the row of pallets, where an open space ran like an alley between the rows for access. She stopped, hand on Angel's head, and aimed the light down the alleyway between the pallets. Lumber gleamed palely in the light, and down toward the far end, something moved.

For an instant her breath caught in her throat. Then she recognized that erect, military posture, the set of strong shoulders. It was Ken. He'd said he and Quinn were taking turns to patrol.

She could slip quietly away. He need never know that she'd been here.

But even as she started to turn, Angel began to bark. Not a soft woof—a full-throated alarm. She felt the dog's muscles bunch under her hand.

Ken whirled toward them at the sound. She had a glimpse of the pale shirt front under his dark jacket. Angel strained against her hand, barking furiously.

"Angel—"

But the rebuke died on her lips. The stack of lumber that loomed over Ken—ten or twelve feet high at least—seemed to shudder. For an instant she thought it was an optical illusion. Then she saw that the whole stack was moving, gaining momentum as it went.

Her cry was lost in Angel's fierce barking. The stack of heavy lumber toppled toward Ken. She saw his startled face, saw his arm flung up to protect his head.

And then the lumber fell, crashing to the ground with a roar that reverberated, shattering the night air with a million echoes.

She couldn't see Ken any longer, just a cloud of dust that billowed into the air like a dense, malignant fog.

FOUR

Angel bounded forward almost before Julianna realized she'd given the signal. She ran after the dog, heart pounding in her throat. Ken—

Please, Lord. Please, Lord. She couldn't seem to verbalize the rest of a prayer, but God surely knew what she meant.

She plunged into the dust cloud, coughing and choking. "Ken! Where are you?"

Angel was already there, barking, nosing at the lumber that had fallen like jackstraws scattered by a giant hand. If Ken was buried under all of that, he'd be badly hurt.

But Angel had focused on the edge of the pile, not the center, and even as Julianna scrambled to the spot, the timbers began to shift. Ken's arm emerged, then his head. He was coughing, but he was conscious and moving.

Thank You, Lord. Thank You.

"Easy. Take it easy." She reached him and clasped his hand. It was warm and vital, and a wave of thankfulness flooded her. "I'll get help."

"No." His hand tightened on hers. "I'm all right. Just help me get out."

"Maybe you shouldn't move."

"I'm fine." His voice was impatient, and he shoved at the nearest timber.

Angel climbed on the pile, nosing a piece of wood away from him, and then licked his face.

Ken patted her. "Okay, Angel. I'm sure my face is dirty. Just give me a minute."

The normality of his tone reassured her. She began pulling two-by-fours away from him. He helped, shoving them until his legs were clear. He got up gingerly, and she reached out a hand to help him out of the pile.

Once on solid ground, he flexed his arms experimentally, winced and rubbed his shoulder. "Ouch. Those two-by-fours pack quite a wallop."

"My car's over by the office. Let me run you over to Vance Memorial to get checked out."

What must it be like to have a hospital named for your family? She couldn't even imagine.

Ken shook his head decisively. "No way. The last thing I need is any doctor getting his hands on me. I've had enough of that the last couple of months."

"But you're hurt—"

"Bumps and bruises. I've felt worse after a game of basketball with my brother." He looked down at his dust-covered clothes. The knee of his jeans was ripped. "I can't go home like this, though. My mother would have hysterics."

Surely he couldn't sound that normal if he were really hurt. She managed a smile, relieved.

"You can clean up in the office. Quinn keeps a stash of clothes there so he can change. He probably has something that will fit you."

He nodded, took a step, and winced again. When she put her arm around his waist, her shoulder under his, he didn't reject the support. They made their way slowly toward the office, Angel circling them.

She had to prop Ken against the door frame while she found the key, but once she had the door open, he moved through without help. She followed, switching on lights.

"Do you want me to call Quinn?"

He paused, frowning. "Not yet. Let me think about it while I get cleaned up. I don't suppose there's any coffee left in that pot."

"I'll make some. Do you need any help?"

Ken's grin broke through, his teeth flashing white in his dust-caked face. "I can get into the shower myself. Thanks anyway, Juli."

The door closed before she could think of a smart retort.

Maybe that was just as well. She busied herself with the coffeemaker, half listening to the drumming of water from the shower in the bathroom on the other side of Quinn's office.

He'd picked up on her grandfather's nickname for her. Juli. She wasn't sure she liked that. It seemed to bring Ken too far into her life, but she didn't know what she could do about it.

About the time the coffee's aroma filled the room, the office door opened. Ken had changed into jeans and a T-shirt she recognized as Quinn's. His hair was wet and tousled from the shower, and the intimacy of the moment made her heart give a little lurch.

She turned away, pouring coffee into mugs. "You'd better figure out some way of hiding that lump on your forehead if you don't want your mother asking embarrassing questions." She carried the mug to him, black, the way he liked it.

He touched the bump gingerly, then finger-combed his hair over it. "How's that?"

She would not stand there looking up into his face. She swung back to get her own mug, adding sugar.

"You'll get by if she doesn't see you in a bright light, but it will probably be purple by morning. How are you going to explain that?"

"I don't know. Bumped it on a door?" He came across the room to take up his favorite perch on the edge of her desk. "I don't make a habit of lying to my mother, but she's been way too nervous about me since I got home. I don't want to give her another reason to tell me I should sit in the house and let her wait on me."

She wouldn't like that herself. "It's natural, I'm afraid. My grandmother's the same way."

He smiled. "Hence the arrival of your grandfather with lunch today."

"Yes." She returned the smile.

The office was perfectly quiet except for the ticking of the round clock that hung over her desk and the muted murmur of the coffeepot. Angel circled twice on the rug and lay down, nose on her paws, watching them.

This was entirely too comfortable—sitting here

alone with Ken, relieved that he was all right. "Did you decide about calling Quinn?"

He frowned, as if he didn't like being reminded about the night's problems. "He'll be coming to relieve me in an hour. I'll talk to him about it then. It's not as if we can do anything in the dark."

"The men will make short work of getting the lumber stacked again once they get here in the morning. But I think you should go on home. I'll wait for Quinn to arrive, if you want."

She didn't think he'd accept that. Sure enough, he was shaking his head before she got the words out.

"No, thanks. I'll hang around." The furrows deepened between his brows. "I wasn't worried about restacking the lumber, though."

She stared at him blankly. "What then?"

He set the mug down on her desk and leaned toward her, face intent. "What made the lumber fall to begin with?"

"Well, I—I don't know." How odd it was, that she hadn't even thought about that. She'd been too focused on Ken's safety.

"Neither do I. But I'm going to find out." When she didn't respond, he shook his head impatiently. "Wake up, Juli. That lumber didn't fall accidentally just when I was walking by."

She rubbed her forehead. "You're right. I don't know why I'm being so stupid. Those stacks are perfectly secure. One couldn't collapse unless—"

"Unless somebody made it happen," he finished for her. His voice was grim.

"More vandalism. But this isn't like putting sugar in the gas tanks. You were hurt." A shudder went through her.

"If Angel hadn't barked when she did, warning me, I would have had more than a few bruises to show for it." His face was grim. "I'd have been buried under that pile of lumber."

Ken pulled into the driveway at his mother's house a couple hours later and frowned at the sight of his brother's car. So much for his hope of sneaking into the house without encountering his mother. All the lights blazed.

What was going on? Usually Mom was ensconced in bed at this hour, half reading, half watching the news on television. He'd counted on just poking his face in long enough to say good-night and beating a quick retreat before she realized anything was wrong.

Quinn wouldn't have called, would he? Or Julianna? Surely not. Well, he better go in and face the music.

It didn't take more than an instant to realize that his accident was, for once, not his mother's preoccupation. His brother, Michael, sat on the sofa, his arm around the shoulders of his girlfriend, Layla Dixou. Both wore a glow that was unmistakable, and if he hadn't figured it out from Mike's expression, he'd have guessed from the fact that his mother was smiling through tears.

He grinned, holding out his hand to Mike. "Let me guess. I need to congratulate you."

Mike stood, his grin threatening to split his lean face. "You'd better. Layla has finally agreed to marry me."

He reached toward her, and the lovely lady vet stood, stepping into the circle of his arm.

"How could I refuse?" She kissed his cheek lightly. "Strange as it seems, I love the guy."

A handshake didn't seem enough. He grabbed his brother in a hug and wrapped his other arm around Layla. He bent to kiss her cheek.

"Welcome. I always wanted another sister."

"Oh my goodness—Holly." Mom wiped tears from her cheeks with both palms. "We have to call and tell her. She'll be so excited."

"You mean she'll be mad that I knew first." Holly, as the elder twin by ten minutes, always wanted to know everything and do everything first.

Mike punched him lightly on the arm. "That's what it is to live at home again, buddy. You get to be first."

Mike meant it as a joke, of course, but it was yet another reminder that other people were getting on with their lives while he was stuck in limbo, waiting. Just waiting.

"Right." He managed a smile, but the stricken look in Mike's eyes told him Mike had realized what he'd said. "Relax, Mike. It's good to be one up on Hol for once."

Mom seemed to have missed that byplay, which was just as well. She caught Layla by the hand, drawing her toward the kitchen. "Come with me to call her, Layla. She'll want to talk to you."

"Hey, won't she want to talk to me?" Mike made a transparent effort to sound hurt.

"Not unless you want to talk about white lace and orange blossoms." Layla patted his cheek. "Consider yourself lucky to miss the girl talk."

Mom and Layla disappeared into the kitchen. Ken had to grin at the expression on Mike's face.

"Hey, didn't you realize that was what was coming next? A wedding, with all the trimmings."

Mike shrugged. "I didn't think. I mean, Layla's kind of unconventional. I thought maybe we'd just get married, not have a big production."

"Layla might let you get away with that, but Mom and Holly certainly wouldn't. Brace yourself, big brother. You're in for it now."

Mike squared his shoulders, as if prepared to face anything. "Well, it's worth it to end up married to Layla. She's one in a million. What she sees in me and a rundown ranch—"

"Guess there's no accounting for tastes." He tried to speak lightly, but there was a lump in his throat. "You're a lucky man."

"I am." Mike said the words as if they were a vow. "You ought to try it, Ken. Quit playing the field and get serious about someone."

"Playing the field is the last thing I've been doing. Trust me, I was too busy to think much about dating. And lately—"

Lately he'd been shuttled from one hospital to another, listening to one Air Force doctor after another.

Mike seemed to pick up on what he didn't say. "Well, you're home now, for awhile at least. Why don't you make some nice Springs woman happy by asking her out?"

"You sound like Holly. Don't tell me you're going to turn into a matchmaker, too?"

Although, come to think of it, he did have a date of

sorts, with Julianna. He'd better not let Holly get wind of that, or she'd never let him forget her efforts.

"No, no." Mike shuddered. "None of that for me. I don't understand heifers, let alone women."

"Well, you've got Layla to take care of that now."

"Right." His face grew serious. "After as close to death as we came in that cave-in, I'm not letting her get away from me. Guess you know it was Julianna Red Feather who found us. Are you seeing anything of her over at the construction company?"

"Some." Mike didn't need to know how much. Or how recently. "I've seen her work with that dog of hers. Pretty impressive, what she does."

"Nobody knows that better than I do." His brow furrowed. "I heard from somebody that coming in after Layla and me was the first time she'd been out with her team since that big hurricane last year in Florida. I guess she went through a pretty bad time there."

It wasn't any of his business, was it? And yet he couldn't help caring about anything that had to do with Julianna.

"I hadn't heard about that, but she's training with her team now. They were out at the construction yard running a drill."

"Good. Seems like something too important to give up." Mike shook his head, smiling. "Funny to think of little Julianna doing that, doesn't it?"

"Five-foot-two inches of nerve and muscle, that's Julianna." She had to have enough courage for three people to do what she did, and he was always intrigued by courage.

"That's who you ought to ask out." Mike reverted with unnerving suddenness to the previous topic. "Mom would be delighted to see you dating Julianna."

"Mom's already delighted enough with your engagement. That'll keep her busy for a while." Who was he kidding? If Mom got wind of him going out with Julianna, he'd never hear the end of it.

"You wish." Mike grinned, obviously pleased at having scored off his little brother. "And speaking of Mom, you'd best do something to hide that lump on your head."

He brushed his hair in his face again. Too bad he still wore it in a regulation military cut. "Better?"

"Just don't let her see you in a bright light. What happened?"

Mike was safe enough, but he didn't want rumors to start spreading about Montgomery Construction. "Not much. Just a little accident down at the construction yard."

Mike snorted. "Seems to me entirely too many 'little accidents' are happening to be accidental."

It was what he'd been thinking himself, but he was startled to hear it from his brother. "What do you mean?"

"I mean I don't believe in coincidence. It'd be nice to think that business with the drug cartel last year was over, but I'm starting to wonder."

Now he was startled. "I thought the ringleader, Escalante, died in a plane crash."

"Never believe everything you hear. They never found his body, and he was the kind that had as many lives as a cat." He shrugged. "Maybe I'm overreacting, but I don't think so. Something's going on." He squeezed Ken's shoulder. "You be careful, you hear?"

Julianna pulled into the parking area at the office early the next morning. She hadn't expected to be able to sleep after Ken's accident the night before, but to her surprise, she'd dived into a deep, dreamless sleep for the first time in a week. She wasn't quite sure what that meant, but at least she'd awakened feeling ready to go.

Somehow she wasn't surprised to see the silver compact Ken drove pull up next to her. Ken wasn't the kind of person who'd take a day off because of a bump on the head.

She got out and stood beside the car, waiting for him to join her. She inspected his forehead.

"Like I said, purple."

He frowned in annoyance. "You sound like my mother."

"Your mother's a very nice lady, but I have no desire to sound like her. What did you and Quinn do after I left last night?"

"Hashed it out without coming to any conclusions." He glanced toward the spot where the lumber lay strewn on the ground. "We'll need to take a good look around in daylight, see if we can find anything. He insisted I go on home. Said he'd make spot checks the rest of the night."

She nodded, getting out her key. "The new man is supposed to start tonight. That should ease the burden."

"Right. Quinn can't expect to stand guard at night and still function during the day. At least they left us alone the rest of the night."

She grasped the door handle, starting to put her key in the lock. But she couldn't. The lock was dented, and the slightest pressure from the key sent the door shifting slightly open.

She exchanged a startled look with Ken. Before she could move he grasped her arm and drew her behind him. Then he shoved the door fully open.

Julianna couldn't suppress a gasp. The office looked as if a small tornado had ripped through it. They'd been wrong. The vandals hadn't left them alone.

For a moment she could only stand and stare. Then fury poured through her. She started toward her desk phone, which lay on the floor on top of the philodendron that had been on the windowsill.

"I'll call the police."

"Wait." Ken's hand on her arm stopped her. He already had his cell phone out, and he pulled her toward the door. "Let me get Quinn first. That decision is his call."

He was right, of course, but even so she itched to be doing something. She leaned against her car, listening while he described the situation to Quinn in a few words. She couldn't make out individual words in Quinn's agitated response, but she thought she got the message.

When Ken hung up, she raised her eyebrows at him.

"No police." He shrugged. "I don't agree with him, but it's his business, not mine. And he's right about one thing—as of tonight, we'll have twenty-four-hour guards on duty."

"I guess I can understand his viewpoint. No one would want to hire a construction company that's a target for vandals. They'd think their property would be next on the list." She moved to the doorway and surveyed the mess. "I guess I'd better get started cleaning this up."

"We," Ken said. "*We* will clean up. And Quinn's on his way."

She nodded and bent to pick up her philodendron. "Poor thing."

"Toss it in the trash," Ken said abruptly. "I'll get you a new one."

She was, quite irrationally, angry. "I don't want a new one. I want *this* one!" She stopped, shaking her head. "Sorry. I didn't mean to snap."

"That's all right. I feel like snapping, too." Ken picked up a trash can. "You decide. You tell me what's safe to throw away."

"Well, the coffee can go, for starters." The contents of the two-pound can had been liberally sprinkled over the mass of papers on the floor. "There's a broom and dustpan in the closet. If you just want to stack the papers, I'll have to go through all of them. Though I probably have everything on my computer."

Ken's gaze narrowed as he transferred his gaze to the computer on her desk. She caught his meaning instantly, and dropped the plant to step over her overturned chair to the desk.

"If they've broken my computer—" But the blue screen appeared, followed by her desktop. "No, thank goodness. That would have been the worst."

"Don't you have everything backed up?" His tone was sharp, and she bristled at the implied criticism.

"I'm backed up for system failure, not vandalism. Who would expect that? But from now on, everything will go home with me on a flash drive backup."

"Right." He ran his hand through his hair, making the purple bruise on his forehead stand out. "I'm sorry. I didn't mean to criticize. Nobody expects something like this. Although—"

She righted her chair. "Although what?"

"Given everything that's been going wrong in the past few months—" He shook his head. "I'm beginning to find it hard to believe there's not something—or someone—behind this sudden rash of misfortune."

Her first impulse was to deny it. People didn't carry on vendettas in placid Colorado Springs. But Ken had a point.

"A lot of bad things have been happening to the Montgomerys and Vances lately," she said slowly.

"Too many bad things." His frown deepened. "Michael thinks it's mixed up with that ugly business last year."

"The drug cartel?" That exposure had been front page news in *The Colorado Springs Sentinel* for months. "I thought they arrested those people."

"Not all of them. And the way things have been going on around here, it seems as if someone's got Montgomery Construction in his gun sight."

She could only stare at him for a long moment. "You're serious?"

"Like I said, I don't believe in coincidence." He shrugged, bending to pick up a handful of papers. "Although I have to admit, this seems like a pretty ineffective way of harassing us."

"Yes," she said slowly, her mind churning with possibilities. She sank down in the desk chair and began paging through her files.

"What are you doing? I thought you were going to help me clean up this mess before we get back to work."

"In a minute."

A bad feeling was growing inside her as she flipped through the files. Ken was right. This was a pretty ineffective way of shutting down a construction company. But if you knew enough, there was a better way.

Ken came to lean over her, hands braced on the back of her chair. She seemed to feel them, as if they were pressed on her shoulders.

"What are you looking for?"

"Something a little more important than spilled coffee."

She opened the report she'd been working on the day before—the latest report on the construction project at the hospital. She paged through it, half-afraid of what she was going to find, her certainty growing.

"There," she said at last. "This is what they were really after."

He bent over her, his breath feathering against her cheek. "What is it?"

"The report Quinn was going to present to the hospital board later today." Today.

"Just looks like rows of figures to me."

"It is." She bit her lip. If she was making a mistake…but she knew in her heart she wasn't. "They've been changed."

"What? How do you know?"

"Because I did this report yesterday. I remember what the numbers should be."

Ken was looking at her with a skeptical expression, and her anger spurted.

"You don't need to look at me that way. I remember the work I've done. And I certainly remember what the figures are supposed to show."

He nodded slowly, and she knew he was accepting her judgment. "So someone tampered with this report. What does it mean?"

She paused, giving herself a moment to question her hunch. But she was right. She knew it.

"If Quinn had presented this report to the hospital board without catching this, it would have looked as if Montgomery Construction were trying to cheat on the contract."

"In other words, that sort of accusation could have meant the end of Montgomery Construction." Ken's hand tightened painfully on her shoulder.

She didn't mind. It made her feel as if she and Ken were united against an enemy. And it began to look as if the feeling was true.

FIVE

"**I**'m not sure what I'm doing here," Julianna murmured as Ken held open the door of the Stagecoach Café for her.

Ken took her arm. "You're here because you're an important part of the company. Besides, this is a council of war, and you know as much about what's been going on as anyone does."

He was probably right about that. She did seem to have been present for the most recent problems, in any event. And Quinn had been almost embarrassingly extravagant in praising her for finding the changes that had been made in the report. She'd spent the rest of the morning closeted in the conference room, reconstituting the report from her notes.

"Seems like a funny place for a council of war, then." She kept her voice low, but the café was nearly deserted in the middle of the afternoon.

"Since Quinn's mother owns it, there couldn't be a safer place." He nodded as a vivacious redhead came bustling toward them, smiling broadly.

"Ken! It's about time you were coming to see me!" She hugged Ken and kissed him loudly on the cheek.

"Good to see you, Fiona." Ken hugged her, but Julianna thought he was a little embarrassed at the greeting. "You know Julianna Red Feather, don't you?"

"Sure thing. Welcome." The smile was extended to her, and then Fiona was turning, gesturing toward the back of the restaurant. "Quinn and Sam are here already. What will you have to drink?"

"Iced tea for me, please," Ken said, and Julianna nodded in agreement.

"Two iced teas coming up." She bustled off.

Ken threaded through small tables covered with red-checked tablecloths. Quinn already sat at the last table in the back, and opposite him was Sam Vance, Ken's cousin and a detective on the Colorado Springs Police Force.

A small shiver went through her. Quinn might insist this was unofficial, but once the police were involved, there was no turning back. She slid into the chair Ken held for her.

Quinn nodded to them, his face grim. "Sam's agreed to meet with us on a strictly off-the-record basis."

"I could have come to the yard and kept it unofficial," Sam said, his tone mild. "We didn't have to go all cloak-and-dagger."

Quinn's frown deepened. "Look, we're just having a nice, quiet lunch together. Anybody who sees us won't think a thing about it. No offense, Sam, but it doesn't do a business any good to get involved with the police."

"That's the thanks I get for serving the public." Sam's

eyes crinkled. "My oldest friends and my family don't want to be seen with me."

"Sam—" Ken's voice held a warning. "This is Quinn's livelihood. We have to let him decide how to handle it."

Fiona appeared just then, carrying a laden tray, and Sam let the subject drop. She began sliding huge bowls of stew in front of them.

"Hope you don't mind," Quinn said. "I thought it would be faster if I just ordered the special all around."

Julianna eyed the puff pastry topping the stew. It was more a dinner than a lunch for her, but she could hardly protest.

Fiona patted her shoulder. "Eat up, honey. You could use a little more meat on those bones."

She managed to smile, and Ken sent her a sympathetic look. After a few more orders to the men to eat hearty, Fiona disappeared back to the kitchen and they were alone.

"Okay, shoot," Sam said, scooping up a spoonful of stew. "Tell me what's going on."

She nibbled at the stew, the rich meaty taste luring her into eating more than she'd intended, while Quinn gave a quick rundown of all the incidents of vandalism that had occurred both at the hospital site and the construction yard.

At the end of Quinn's recitation, Sam put down his fork. "You don't need me to tell you it's the kind of thing that can happen to any construction company." His face was guarded, and she couldn't tell what he was thinking.

"Right," Quinn said. "If it hadn't been for all the other inexplicable things that have been happening to the Vance and the Montgomery families. And if it hadn't been for last night's episode."

He nodded to Ken, who took up the story then.

She watched Ken's face as he talked. The lines seemed deeper this afternoon, and the way he rubbed his forehead from time to time suggested that he had another of the headaches he didn't want to admit to. He ought to be resting and recuperating instead of being plunged headlong into trouble, but she didn't suppose he'd agree to that.

Sam's expression grew graver as he listened to the account of Ken's close call. "You're sure it couldn't have happened accidentally?"

"It was no accident." Quinn seemed to be grinding his teeth. "Those lumber pallets could no more collapse by themselves than they could take flight."

She suddenly found herself the focus of Sam's intent gaze, and her nerves jumped. "What about you, Julianna? Any hint that someone else was there?"

She thought back carefully before answering. "I didn't see anything, no. But I think Angel, my dog, must have heard something. She gave an alarm bark before the lumber started to move. I didn't think about it at the time, but I don't see what else it could have been. She sensed someone there."

Sam nodded. "Did she try to chase after him, whoever it was?"

"No, but she wouldn't. Ken was trapped. All her training would send her straight after him."

Her heart clenched at the image that formed in her mind—the huge stack of lumber, the dust rising from it, the panic she'd felt when she realized Ken was somewhere underneath.

"Right." Sam glanced from one face to the other. "How did he get in?"

"When I made the rounds, one of the gates was standing ajar," Ken said, his voice expressionless. "We certainly hadn't left it that way."

"Well, not that I don't value my cousin's life and limb, but that still could have been an act of vandalism gone awry. After all, he couldn't have known you'd be in that place at that time."

"Agreed. That could have been a crime of opportunity," Ken said, his voice dry. "But what Julianna found this morning couldn't. Tell him, Juli."

She saw Sam shoot a quick, speculative glance at his cousin when Ken used her nickname. Then he focused on her, and her mouth was suddenly dry.

"Ken and I were the first ones at the office this morning. We found the place turned upside-down. At first it looked as if the computers hadn't been touched, but then I checked mine out. I found that someone had tampered with a report I was doing for Quinn to present to the hospital board."

"And let me tell you," Quinn said, his voice hard, "if I'd walked into the hospital board with that report, you'd be seeing the end of Montgomery Construction. We wouldn't be able to survive losing that contract, not after the losses from the fire."

"I'd like to see the file." Sam held up his hand to quiet

Quinn's protest. "Nothing official, I know. But Julianna can make a copy for me, can't she?"

She shot a look at Quinn, and he nodded permission.

"I'll make a copy. And I'll also get you a copy of my original file, so you can see what was changed. It was really very subtle. Whoever did it, he or she knew what they were doing."

"Not your typical teenage vandal, then," Sam said.

She sensed, rather than felt, Ken stiffen, and knew he was thinking of Jay.

"Certainly not," she said firmly.

"Well?" Quinn frowned at Sam. "What's the verdict?"

Sam shook his head slowly. "I can't dismiss it, not with all the things that have been happening. It's almost as if Escalante has come back from the grave to start a vendetta against us."

"If he was ever in the grave," Quinn said.

"I've been wondering that myself, but all I can do is investigate." Sam's face was grim. "And suggest that you add more security. Any of you have anything else to add?"

She held her breath. If Ken mentioned Jay—

"I hate to bring this up," Ken said, not looking at her. "But there's a kid, Jay Nieto, who's been in the construction yard, helping Julianna with her search-and-rescue team training."

"That's ridiculous," she snapped. "Jay wouldn't do anything like that, and he doesn't have the knowledge necessary to falsify my computer records that way."

She glared at Ken, anger churning in her stomach. He had no right to bring Jay into this.

"You're the one who said how bright he is. Look, I

know how you feel about the kid, but if he's under the influence of that gang leader—"

"What gang leader?" Sam's voice cut like a knife.

"He's not a gang member," she protested. "He's just a lonely kid looking for someone to accept him." But Sam was still waiting for an answer. "Theo Crale," she said reluctantly.

Sam drew in a breath. "The Posse. We don't have enough on them to bring anyone down, but I'm convinced they're on the fringe of the drug trade."

Her heart sank. "Jay wouldn't."

"Look, I'm not suggesting having the police haul the kid in for questioning." Ken leaned toward her across the table, his level gaze holding hers, and it was as if they were alone. "I just want you to set up a chance for me to talk with him. Get a sense of the boy informally." He glanced toward Sam. "That okay with you?"

"Since everything we've said has been informal, I guess I have to agree."

Ken zeroed in on her again. "Juli?"

She didn't have a choice, did she? "All right. I'll set something up."

She'd do it. But she wasn't going to forgive Ken easily for this.

The woman strolled casually across the park, her heels clicking on the concrete walkway. Anyone who really knew her would be aware that she wasn't the type to take walks in the park for pleasure, but then, no one in her current life really knew her.

Battalion Chief Neil O'Brien already sat on the

bench she'd specified, flipping nervously through the pages of the daily newspaper. His foot tapped against the pavement in a broken rhythm.

She felt a fresh spurt of annoyance. The man was the worst conspirator in the world. It would be obvious to any interested observer that he was up to no good.

Fortunately, no one in the park this spring afternoon showed any interest in O'Brien. The man had managed to stay out of sight since the fire at Montgomery Construction put him under suspicion—she had to give him that. But he was scared and he was nervous, and Escalante was a fool to trust him with anything, in her opinion.

"Hurry up," he said, as soon as she got within earshot. He sent a nervous glance around.

She slowed her pace deliberately. He couldn't be permitted to think he could give her orders about anything. She sat at the far end of the bench, gazing across the park. She didn't have to look at O'Brien to know he was afraid. He positively reeked of fear.

"You should have picked a less public place." He had sense enough to keep the paper up in front of his face. "I'll be spotted."

"Don't be an idiot. No one knows or cares who you are."

"But—"

"You messed up that attack on Kenneth Vance. He's fine. What made you attempt such a thing?"

The newspaper trembled. "*El Jefe* wants him dead— I know that. I saw a chance and I took it." A whining note entered his voice. "It's not my fault it didn't come off. If that fool woman and her dog hadn't been there to warn him, the Chief would be praising me right now."

"I doubt very much that the Chief will praise you for anything. He may want the man dead, but it has to look like an accident. Is that understood?"

"Yes," he mumbled.

"Very well. Here are your orders. You are to step up the vandalism, but keep it at a level that they won't want to bring the police in. Understand? They are not to suspect any connection with the fires."

He nodded sullenly.

"Watch for a chance to eliminate Kenneth Vance," she said. "But bear in mind it has to look like an accident."

"I don't want—"

"What you want doesn't matter in the least." She didn't trouble to hide her disgust for him. "You will do as you're told."

"I was just going to say I've found the perfect tool to carry out the vandalism." He sounded sulky.

"Fine, but see that he does exactly as he's told. *El Jefe* is becoming tired of excuses. He won't tolerate any more." She stood, still not looking at him. "So you'd better be very sure you're following orders, or your pretty little wife will be planning your funeral."

She turned away, gratified to see that the newspaper shook in his hands. She didn't have any illusions about O'Brien. If he were caught, he'd hand over her name, since it was the only one he knew.

But Escalante wouldn't let him live long enough to

do that, in any event. And with any luck, the next blow to the Vance family would be a deadly one.

"You two can set up the ladder and plank right over there." Julianna indicated a level spot in the debris area.

Ken smiled at Jay and got a cautious smile in return. "I guess she means us, Jay. I don't see anyone else around to tote things for her."

Jay lifted one end of the ladder. "We did this setup once before. I know how it goes."

"You're the boss then." He picked up the other end of the ladder and let the kid lead the way.

In response to his prodding, Julianna had hired Jay to help set up another training event at Montgomery Construction. But this time he was going to be Juli's assistant. If an hour of working with the kid didn't tell him what he needed to know about the boy's character, then he'd wasted a lot of time as an Air Force officer.

The kid was no shirker, he had to give him that up front. He was quick to take the heavy part of any load as they began setting up the ladders, planks and tunnels.

Ken tested the first ladder, making sure it was steady. Quinn wouldn't thank him if someone got hurt here.

"Your volunteers have to prove they can climb a ladder, is that it?"

Julianna looked down at him from above, where she was setting a plank into place. "We're not testing the volunteers, although their agility is important, too. This particular exercise is for the dogs."

He blinked, surveying the ladder. "The dogs can climb ladders?"

"Sure they can." Jay's smile was more natural now. "I didn't believe it at first either, but they do." He patted Angel, who pressed against his leg, raising her black-muzzled head to give him a grave, intelligent look.

Julianna would probably say that the dog's instincts about the boy were proof enough for her. Ken needed a little more, though.

"So, has working with Juli and her team made you want to start training a dog of your own?" He raised another plank over his head, and Jay scrambled up the ladder to take it.

"I wouldn't mind having a dog." Jay sounded a little wistful. "I did when we lived at the pueblo, but my dad says there's not room in our apartment. When he's making enough money to buy a house, he says we can get one."

There was a trace of something in the boy's voice— as if he wanted to believe what his father told him but didn't quite dare.

"Do you like living in The Springs?"

Jay shrugged. "It's okay. I want to be with my dad."

"I lost my dad a few years ago, but I still enjoy spending some time here with the rest of my family."

He'd have to open up a bit to the kid if he expected anything in return. Julianna was a few feet away, her back to them, ostensibly absorbed in unpacking equipment, but he didn't doubt that she heard every word.

"It must get boring, though," Jay said. "I'll bet you want to get back on active duty."

Jay's innocent words struck him straight in the heart. What had he just been thinking about, opening up to the kid? This was more open than he wanted to be, but he didn't have much choice.

"Yeah, I guess it does get a little claustrophobic sometimes. When you love what you do, you don't want to be away from it."

The longing went through him, sharp as a knife. He wanted to be flying again, cutting through the sky without a thought for anything except the perfection of the machine and the completion of the mission.

Jay tested the stability of the plank with a quick jerk. "If I could fly, I don't figure I'd want to ever do anything else."

"No. You wouldn't." He fought to control his voice. No one needed to know how much this meant to him. "Not if that's what you're destined to do."

Jay looked upward, and Ken knew without looking what he saw. Sharp mountain ridges against an incredibly blue sky. The contrails of jets etching a pattern on the blue. Air Force blue. You didn't get away from that in Colorado Springs, home of the Academy.

Maybe he'd have been better off recuperating anywhere else but here. Still, where else would he go? His years of devotion to his career had left him without ties, except for the ones he'd been born to.

"I thought maybe I'd enlist after high school. If they'd take me. I know they don't take just anybody." Jay scrambled back down the ladder.

"Julianna seems to think you have what it takes to do more than that. She says you're pretty smart."

The boy shrugged, not looking at him. "Yeah, well, that doesn't matter. You don't get into the Academy just by being smart."

So that was the boy's secret dream. He'd have to tread carefully here, if he didn't want all those barriers going up again.

"It's a good thing that's not the only consideration, or I probably wouldn't have gotten in." He managed a grin. "I didn't always burn up the books when I was in school, but when I figured out what I had to do to get what I wanted, I managed to try a little harder."

Jay's dark gaze studied him with an intensity that was unsettling. "You weren't Pueblo."

A spark of anger ignited, and he grabbed Jay's arm. The kid jerked back instinctively, but he didn't let go.

"Listen, don't use that as an excuse—not to me, and certainly not to yourself. Your heritage won't keep you out, but your attitude might. The Academy cares about what you can do and what kind of stuff you're made of inside. Not what color you are."

The kid's gaze dropped. "Yeah, well, maybe that's true, but there's all that stuff about getting recommended and everything. I couldn't do that. Who'd recommend me?"

That was the bottom line for Jay, he realized suddenly. The kid figured no matter what he did, he wouldn't have what he perceived as the pull necessary to get in. He didn't realize how wrong he was.

"Believe me, Jay. If you have what the Academy wants, people will line up to recommend you."

"Yeah, right." He turned away, obviously not believing Ken's words.

"I mean it." His hand tightened on the boy's shoulder. "I'll promise you something. Wherever I am, whatever I'm doing, you come to me when you're ready to apply, and if you've done your part, I'll see to it that you get everything else you need."

Jay studied him again, and he realized he wasn't the only one who was trying to take someone's measure today. "Juli thinks you're okay."

In other words, Juli's opinion counted more with Jay than Ken's status as an Air Force pilot. Well, that was okay. In fact, that was fine.

"Seems like Juli's someone you can trust."

"Are you kidding? Juli and her grandparents are the best." The boy's voice warmed. "I gotta believe what she says."

"You know what? I do, too."

He realized suddenly that it was true. His instincts were telling him the same thing Juli had—that this boy wouldn't do anything to hurt her.

He patted the boy's shoulder. "So you keep in touch with her. When I go back on duty—" *When*, not *if*. He had to believe that. "—I'll let her know where to find me. And when you're ready, I'll do everything I can to help you."

Jay didn't say anything, but he nodded. And Ken could almost believe that was hope in his eyes.

He glanced toward Juli. "Come on. Guess we'd better find out what the boss wants us to do next."

When they reached her, Juli handed them something that looked like baseball bases. He hefted one. "Do the dogs play baseball, too?"

"Smart guy." She smiled, but he could see the

wariness behind that smile. She wasn't quite ready to forgive him yet for bringing up Jay's name with the police. "They probably could, if they put their minds to it. We need to set up the bases for stop and stay."

"Stop and stay?"

"It's a test of a dog's direct-ability. The dog has to respond instantly to commands given from a distance. That could save his life on a disaster site."

"Looks like Jay has done this before." The boy was moving away from them, already setting up the bases, apparently knowing how far apart to put them.

She nodded. "We do this fairly often in training. He's a sharp kid. You don't have to show him how to do something more than once."

"I believe that." He'd caught the boy's quick intelligence at work in even a casual conversation. "Sometimes he lets his attitude get in the way."

"Is that what you told him?" Her face tightened a little.

"No. I told him that if he still wants the Air Force Academy when it's time to apply that I'd do everything I can to help him."

"You did?" The squeak of astonishment in Julianna's voice showed him how little she'd expected that of him. "You mean that?"

"I'm not in the habit of making promises I don't mean."

She studied him for a moment. "You talked to him about the Academy. I know that can't have been easy."

"Easy? No." He wanted to deny the sympathy in her eyes. How did she know so clearly what would hurt him? "But you were right about him. That's what he dreams of."

"Did you tell him those dreams could come true?"

"I told him the truth. It's not easy to get into the Academy. They have their choice of the best and the brightest. But if that's what he wants, he has as good a chance of making it as anyone."

"I find it hard to believe you'd encourage him if you believed him capable of vandalism."

She stood close to him, her head tilted back so that she could look up into his face. The sunlight gilded her cheeks with bronze, and he wanted to touch her skin, to see if it was as warm and smooth and alive as it looked.

He was suddenly aware of the strength of her—not just physical, although that was there, but an inner, spiritual strength that didn't depend upon what anyone else thought of her.

He wanted her to look at him with approval, even admiration. But he wouldn't get that by glossing over what he had to say to her.

"I see the same thing you see in him, Juli. He's bright, and he has courage and determination. I agree that he wouldn't intentionally do anything to hurt you."

Her expression seemed to harden, as if he were looking at a bronze statue of her instead of a living, breathing, vulnerable woman. "I sense a 'but' coming."

He nodded. "But would he realize that vandalism here would hurt you? I don't know."

"He would." Her eyes flashed fire. "And he wouldn't do that."

"I hope you're right." His hand closed over her wrist, and he felt her pulse pound against his palm. "I want to believe you're right. My instincts agree with yours. But I can't totally trust my instincts, or yours, where someone else's livelihood is at stake. I can't."

SIX

Several days had passed, and nothing more had happened at the construction company. Julianna took her seat in the church parlor for Bible study, nodding to those around her. She'd deliberately come in at the last possible moment, hoping to avoid any uncomfortable conversation with Ken.

Maybe it wasn't right to say nothing had happened recently. Ken had been avoiding her again—that was what was happening. It was as if, after their conversation at the training setup, he'd decided they were getting too close.

She understood that feeling, and she agreed that a little distance between them was probably a good idea. He hadn't liked letting her see how much it bothered him to talk to Jay about an Air Force career.

And she hadn't liked the feeling that she was conspiring with him against Jay. She shifted restlessly in the metal folding chair. Pastor Gabriel was deep in conversation with an elderly woman who sat on the burgundy love seat that made up the first ring of the circle of seats, and apparently he wasn't ready to start yet.

Surely Ken couldn't believe Jay was involved in the vandalism. She had to cling to the hope that Ken wouldn't have offered to help Jay get into the Academy if he thought the boy had trashed the office or tried to dump a load of lumber on his head.

Maybe the fact that the vandal hadn't struck since that last incident was making everyone nervous. She agreed with Quinn about that—tampering with the hospital report wasn't a simple act of vandalism. It was an attack against the company's very existence. Ken couldn't believe Jay did that. The very idea was ridiculous.

She had to clear the air with Ken. Avoiding the subject wasn't helping. Even as she had the thought, the door opened and Ken and Holly came in. As if their arrival had been a signal, Pastor Gabriel opened his Bible.

Holly and Ken slid into the chairs next to her. She nodded to them, and forced her attention to Pastor Gabriel.

The subject of the study was one of her favorite passages—Psalm 27. "The Lord is my light and my salvation; whom should I fear? The Lord is the refuge of my life; of whom should I be afraid?"

She let the words seep into her heart. They were a promise she needed to remember.

Next to her, she felt Holly move restlessly. Beyond Holly, Ken kept his gaze fixed on the pastor, his profile stern and withdrawn.

After the study, she promised herself. She'd find some way to talk to him about Jay.

But when the moment came, Ken got up so quickly that it seemed the final "Amen" had released a spring. He turned away, as if to make a quick escape, but the end of the row was blocked by several people greeting each other. His left hand, with its gold Academy ring, clenched on the back of a chair, and she felt his tension as if they were touching.

Maybe that conversation she'd hoped to have would have to wait. She couldn't—

Holly started to get up. She let out a gasp. The small sound had Julianna turning to her instantly. Holly sank back onto the chair, her face white. She met Julianna's gaze and shook her head.

"Get Ken," she whispered.

Alarm threading along her nerves, Julianna moved carefully past her friend and scurried to the end of the row of chairs, where Ken was anchored by a couple of elderly ladies carrying on an animated conversation.

"Ken," she said softly. Holly obviously didn't want to draw attention to herself.

He turned slightly toward her. "Hi, Julianna."

She touched his arm, lowering her voice. "Holly needs you."

In an instant the armor she'd sensed him holding against her dropped. He shoved a chair out of his way to reach his sister, Julianna right behind him.

"What is it, Holly?" He knelt next to her, his voice low.

"Hurts." Holly reached out to grab Julianna's hand and hold on tight. "I don't want everyone to know and make a fuss over me. Just help me out to the car."

"Pull up to the vestibule door," Julianna said quickly. "That'll be the easiest way to take her out. I'll stay with her."

His face drawn with concern, Ken nodded. He stood and hurried to the door.

Pastor Gabriel looked toward them and seemed to take in the situation with a glance. He ushered the last stragglers out of the parlor and came to them, his face drawn with concern.

"What can I do?" He clasped their linked hands in his.

Holly managed a smile. "Pray."

"I'm already doing that," he said. "Are you going to the emergency room?"

She nodded.

"I'll follow you."

Before he could say more, Ken hurried back in. "I'm right outside," he said. He bent over his sister. "I'm going to carry you to the car."

Ignoring her protest, he lifted her carefully in his arms. Julianna grabbed her bag and Holly's and hurried to open the door. In seconds, it seemed, they had Holly secured in the passenger seat. She was still gripping Julianna's hand, so Juli slipped into the seat behind her.

Ken backed out the walkway he'd brought the car in and turned onto the street. She could sense the urgency in him, but he maneuvered the vehicle as cautiously as if he were transporting a wedding cake.

"Be there in a jiffy," he said. He glanced at Holly, so concentrated on his twin that Julianna had the feeling he'd forgotten she was there. "I know twins are supposed to share each other's pains, but can I miss this one?"

"Chicken," Holly said, and her smile flickered.

Through their clasped hands, Julianna seemed to feel the comfort Holly received from her brother's words. She patted Holly's fingers.

"Can you tell us what you're feeling?"

"Pain." Holly's grip tightened. "Take-your-breath-away pain, down very low in my belly. If something's wrong with the baby—"

"We're almost there," Ken said quickly. The car spurted up the drive to the hospital. "Hang on, Hol. They'll take good care of you."

Indeed, the moment Ken pulled to a stop outside the emergency room door, a wheelchair was there. Attendants whisked Holly toward an exam room. Since Holly still gripped her hand, Julianna went, too.

When the nurse helped Holly onto the exam table, she grimaced and then tried to smile at Ken.

"No offense, Ken, but I'd rather you weren't here for this examination. Julianna will stay with me. Why don't you go call Jake?"

It flickered through Juli's mind to wonder if Ken resented her supplanting him, but if anything, he looked relieved.

"I'll have to call Mom, too, or she'll never forgive us."

Holly nodded. "Try not to alarm her."

Ken managed a smile. "I'm afraid that's beyond my capabilities, but I'll try." He glanced at Julianna, and she saw the pain he was trying to hide. "Take care of her."

She nodded, throat tightening.

No sooner had Ken left than Holly's obstetrician arrived. The tall, gray-haired woman brought an aura of calm and control with her into the room.

"Dr. Smithfield." The relief in Holly's voice was obvious. "The baby's okay, isn't she?"

"We'll soon see." Dr. Smithfield touched Holly's abdomen, and Holly seemed to relax at her touch. "Suppose we have your friend wait outside for just a few minutes, all right?"

Holly nodded, so Julianna slipped out, making her way to the waiting room. Pastor Gabriel was already there, but in answer to his raised brow, all she could do was shake her head.

"I don't know anything yet. Her obstetrician is with her now."

"Then we'll pray." He clasped her hands in his, seeming oblivious of the receptionist behind the desk, and lifted his voice in prayer.

By the time he'd finished, Ken came back in, slipping a cell phone into his pocket. "Anything?"

"Not yet. Did you reach her husband?"

He nodded. "He'll be here in a couple of minutes. His parents will stop by for Mom."

They were about to be invaded by a horde of Montgomerys and Vances, in other words. Well, that was natural. Holly had linked the two families when she married Jake Montgomery, formalizing the ties that had existed between them for several generations.

She didn't belong here, with people like that. But she couldn't leave until she knew that Holly was all right.

Please, Father. Protect her and the baby.

By the time Dr. Smithfield emerged from the exam room, the waiting room had filled up with Montgomerys and Vances, and Pastor Gabriel had launched an informal prayer service.

The waiting room fell silent when Dr. Smithfield entered. She smiled. "You can all stop worrying. Holly and the baby are both fine."

"Thank Heaven," Jake said fervently, running a hand through dark blond hair. "Can I see her?"

She nodded. "Go on in. She'll tell you all about it."

Ken's mother took a quick step forward as if to follow, but Dr. Smithfield cut her off smoothly.

"Holly asked me to explain the situation, so you'd all relax and stop worrying. It's nothing unusual. The baby has shifted to a position where she's pressing on a nerve. The situation is very painful for the mother, but there's no danger."

"But can't you do something for Holly?" Marilyn Vance was obviously concerned for her baby.

"We've given her something, and she's much more comfortable already," Dr. Smithfield soothed. "I'm going to keep her overnight, just to be on the safe side. You can see her once she's in her room, all right?"

Mrs. Vance looked as if there were a protest on her lips, but Ken took hold of her arm.

"That's fine, Doctor. Thank you." He seemed to send an unspoken signal to his aunt, and the woman came to put her arm around his mother.

"Let's get some coffee while you're waiting, Marilyn." She led her to a chair.

Now she had no excuse to stay. Holly was going to

be all right, and she was surrounded by people who loved her. Julianna Red Feather didn't belong here with people like the Montgomerys and the Vances.

She slipped toward the door, but just as she went out, she realized that Ken had followed. He caught her hand, bringing her to a halt just outside the door, where they stood bathed in a pool of light from the emergency room sign.

Ken inhaled. "Smells better out here. I hate the smell of hospitals. You don't think Holly could tell, do you?"

She was unaccountably touched. "She was just grateful you were there. I just hadn't realized—" She stopped, thinking she was getting too close again.

"Realized what?" Ken captured her hand in his, so that she couldn't move away.

"The link between you two. I guess all those things they say about twins are true."

"Funny. I hadn't thought about that in ages, but I guess so." His fingers were warm around her wrist. "I've been away too long. Maybe it's right that I'm here now." He frowned. "Although if that's the case, God could have used a less painful way of getting me home."

It sounded as though Ken were searching for answers to the puzzling question of God's will, just as she was. She had to say something, although she certainly wasn't an expert.

"I don't believe—well, that God caused your crash just so you'd be here. But I want to believe that God can bring something good out of the most terrible things."

She had to believe that, or she'd have no way to keep on going.

"That sounds like personal experience talking." Ken's voice was low.

She tried to smile. "Something like that."

"Will you tell me about it someday?"

"I don't know." He was the one person who might understand, but she didn't think they'd ever be close enough for that.

He squeezed her hand. "I hope so, Juli. I really do."

His voice was so warm that it brought her gaze, startled, to meet his. Her breath caught. Ken was looking at her as if they meant something to each other. As if—

A flicker of panic went through her. She couldn't feel anything for Ken. She couldn't.

But she did.

"I think it's about time we left Jake and Holly alone." Ken nodded toward the hospital room door. "Come on, everyone out."

"Ken's right." Jake's father put his arm around his wife. "Come on, Liza. Jake and Holly don't need us right now."

Liza bent over the bed to drop a kiss on Holly's cheek. "You call us if you need anything." She gave her son a stern look. "Anything at all."

"We will, Mom." Jake released Holly's hand long enough to hug her. "I'll give you a call in the morning."

Ken nudged his mother. "Come on, Mom. Us, too."

His mother frowned. "If you mean that we should leave also, Kenneth, please say so."

When Mom started correcting his speech, she wasn't worrying too much. He smiled, bending over to kiss his sister.

"'Night, Hol."

"Thanks for clearing the room," she whispered.

He grinned. "Hey, I didn't need the twin thing to figure that one out. You behave. We'll check in tomorrow."

"Tell Julianna I said thanks."

"Will do."

Julianna. They had felt closer than he'd have dreamed possible in those moments when they'd stood outside the E.R. together. For an instant he'd thought of lowering his head to kiss her soft mouth.

That would have been a mistake. But he couldn't help wishing he'd done it.

Of course it took a few more minutes to actually get his mother outside the room. They paused in the hallway, and he realized how exhausted his mother looked. This had taken a toll on her.

"Do you need me to drive you home?" he asked.

"I have my car. But there is something else you can do."

"Name it."

"Go with me to see your uncle Max." Her hand closed over his. "I know it's late, but the nurses will let us go in."

"Sure." He tried to smile, even though the thought of Uncle Max, lying in a coma, had him wanting to run the other way. "Lead on."

His mother led the way through a maze of hospital corridors as if she spent half her time here.

"Do you come to see Uncle Max often?"

"Of course." She looked surprised. "Usually every other day."

"But he doesn't know you're here."

His mother paused, her hand on a patient room door. "Maybe. Maybe not. But *I* know."

It was an unexpected insight into his mother that left him speechless for a moment. He'd been underestimating her strength.

Fortunately she didn't seem to expect any response. She pulled the door open and stepped inside, motioning for him to follow.

He entered reluctantly, realizing that this was the first time he'd come to the hospital since he'd returned home. That suddenly seemed shameful.

His mother had already approached the bed and bent over, taking his uncle's hand in hers. "Guess who's dropped in to see you, Max? Ken is here."

He stepped closer, his stomach clenching. The man lying on the hospital bed, connected to all those tubes and monitors, couldn't possibly be Uncle Max. Max was tall, strong, vibrant, with a hearty laugh that made anyone who heard him want to laugh, too. He couldn't be the pale, motionless figure on the bed with the sheet and light blue bedspread folded neatly across his chest.

"Say something, Ken," his mother murmured. "Talk to him."

He looked at her helplessly. "What? He can't hear me."

"You don't know that." His mother gave him the severe look she'd once given recalcitrant high school students. "Many doctors say that a patient in a coma may be able to hear, even though he can't respond. Now talk to him."

The command in her eyes made him feel about six years old again. He touched the lax hand, somehow surprised that it was warm.

"Hey, Uncle Max." His throat choked on the words, and he knew, suddenly, why he hadn't come to the hospital before this. He was afraid. He saw too many reminders of his own weakness here.

"Ken's home on medical leave," his mother said chattily. "But you knew that. I already told you. It's just so good to have him here."

"Good to be home, too." He forced his voice to something approaching normal. "Mom's been cooking all my favorite meals for me."

"God brought Ken home safely," his mother said softly. "He'll bring you back to us, too."

Something deep inside him seemed to crack at her words. How had he gotten so selfish, so absorbed in his own problems, that he didn't notice other people were hurting, too?

"That's right, Uncle Max. You'll be back with us soon. Mom and Holly are planning a big bash to celebrate Michael's engagement. You don't want to miss that."

"Remember how we used to think we'd never get these kids of ours married off?" His mother sounded perfectly normal. "It looks like it's finally happening. Now if Ken would just find a nice girl—"

"Come on, Mom. Uncle Max doesn't want to hear that." He was as bad as she was, talking as if his uncle could hear, could respond—

Max's hand moved. For an instant Ken thought he was imagining things, and then it happened again. His hand moved, wrapping around Ken's.

"Mom?"

She looked across the hospital bed at him, and her

eyes filled with tears. "It's happening," she whispered, her voice trembling. "He's beginning to wake up."

Julianna frowned at the array of plants on her windowsill a few days later. Ken hadn't mentioned anything about her poor demolished philodendron, but she'd come in one morning to find a veritable garden of potted plants on the windowsill. No note, but she knew he'd done it.

She hadn't seen much of Ken since then. Maybe that wasn't surprising. With Holly needing extra help and the whole Vance clan delirious over the mayor's progress in recovering from his coma, he probably hadn't even thought of her.

Well, maybe it was better to be ignored that way. That night at the hospital had been disturbing enough. Her cheeks had burned all the way home at the thought of how close they'd come to kissing.

And she'd been doubly embarrassed to realize her car hadn't been at the hospital lot so she couldn't make a fast retreat. She'd had to hitch a ride back to the church with Pastor Gabriel to retrieve it.

That had been quite an astonishing turn of events—Max Vance beginning to come out of his coma just at that time. According to rumor, he wasn't totally cognizant of things around him yet, but it had to be a hopeful sign. She paused long enough for a quick prayer.

Remember Your servant, Maxwell Vance, Father. Be with him and his family, and bless him with a return to health.

The office was empty and quiet. Almost too quiet.

They hadn't even had any attention from their vandal in the past few days.

Still, it paid to be cautious. She dropped her flash drive backup in her handbag and started for the door. No one would get their hands on her files again.

As for Ken, it was probably best that he'd been too busy to be around—hopefully too busy to remember that the powwow was tomorrow night.

She wouldn't remind him. Given her unfortunate reaction to him, it was better that way. She switched on the alarm, stepped outside and locked the door. She turned around and saw Ken's car pulling in next to hers.

Her heart gave a little flutter, reminding her that she wasn't immune to him.

Ken slid out of the car, leaving the motor running. "Hi, Juli. I hoped I'd be in time to catch you."

She wouldn't assume his reasons were personal, rather than business. "Was there something you needed me to do?"

He looked momentarily confused. "No. I wanted to thank you again for all your help the other night."

She shook her head, smiling. "I just held Holly's hand, that's all."

"No, that wasn't all. You kept her calm." He grinned. "Kept me calm, too. I don't know what I'd have done if she'd been in labor."

"With any luck, when that happens it will be her husband's job."

"Right." A shadow crossed his face. "It's hard to say where I'll be by then."

The reminder that his time here was brief hurt more

than it should, and she tried to find something to say that wouldn't reveal her feelings.

"I heard about your uncle. How is he doing?"

"Making progress." Ken leaned back against his car's fender, seeming prepared to stay and talk indefinitely. The yard was quiet, with most of the workers gone, and the low hum of traffic from the road beyond the fence was the only sound. "He seems to recognize everyone, although he's not communicating much yet. But the doctors are pleased, and my aunt's holding on to hope for a full recovery."

"Is that a reasonable hope?"

He shrugged. "Apparently there's no way of being sure."

"He's been in my prayers." Maybe that was a good way of making her exit. She turned toward her car. "Well, I'd better get home before Angel thinks I've forgotten her."

"Wait a sec." Ken touched her arm lightly, stopping her. "We haven't made arrangements for tomorrow night yet."

"Tomorrow night?" She tried to look blank, but suspected she didn't pull it off. So he hadn't forgotten the powwow after all.

"The powwow. Remember?"

"I thought since you've been so busy with family, that maybe you didn't have time for that." And it would probably be better for her emotional health if that were the case.

"Not a chance," he said. "I've been looking forward to it. What time shall I pick you up?"

"I could meet you—"

He was already shaking his head. "I always pick up my dates."

She could tell by the glint in his eye that he expected her to object to the term, so she didn't. "Make it seven. That should give us plenty of time to drive up to the park."

"Seven it is." He turned away, and this time it was her turn to call him back.

"Aren't you forgetting something? You don't know where I live."

"No, you've forgotten." His lips twitched. "I'm head of security around here. I know where everyone lives."

Smiling in apparent satisfaction at having the last word, he swung into his car, waved and pulled away.

SEVEN

"So this is a powwow."

Ken pulled into a parking place in a long row of cars and pickups. Julianna had said very little on the drive up the mountain to the park where the powwow was being held. Maybe if he needled her a little, he'd get a reaction.

"This is a parking lot." She frowned at him. "As I suspect you know very well."

"Hey, just trying to get you to say something. Shouldn't you be giving me a ton of background information, so I don't make any mistakes?"

She opened the door and slid out without waiting for him. She bent to look in the car at him, her black braids swinging down. Her lips twitched in what might have been a smile. "If I see you about to make any big blooper, I'll head you off. Maybe."

"Wow, thanks a lot. Does the powwow have a bouncer who will throw me out if I don't behave properly?"

He got out, rounding the car to join her. Julianna might not come up to his shoulders, but he was the novice here, while she was on her own turf.

He'd picked right when he'd decided to wear jeans and a western shirt, apparently. Julianna's embroidered shirt was tucked into her jeans and a glint of turquoise-and-silver showed at her throat. A belt with an ornamental buckle, again in turquoise-and-silver, spanned her slim waist.

"No, they'll let me do that. This way." She nodded toward a path that led uphill. In the distance he could hear the muffled thump of drums, and above them the sun sank behind the mountain in a fiery display that painted the sky in orange and purple.

"I'd like to see you try." He put one hand on her shoulder as they walked up the path, emphasizing the difference in size between them.

Juli tossed her head, the black braids swinging. "I can't pick on you when you're—" She stopped abruptly, but he knew what she'd been going to say.

"When I'm on the disabled list," he finished for her, managing to say the words evenly. "I don't need two good eyes for that. Just for—"

Now it was his turn to stop and wish the words unsaid. Was he ever going to get over the feeling that an unwary step would send him into a dark chasm?

"Just for flying," she said softly. "I'm sorry, Ken. I didn't mean to remind you."

"It's okay." To his surprise, it was. "To tell you the truth, I don't mind when you say something about it. I just can't talk to my family about it. So they tiptoe around my feelings."

She nodded. "I know. They care too much, and you don't want to hurt them."

"That's it exactly. It sounds like you've been in that situation, too."

She shrugged, her face averted. "I guess I have."

He wanted to ask her to tell him about whatever put that somber look in her eyes, but he couldn't. He didn't have the right to pry.

He frowned, trying to get a handle on what he felt for Julianna. At first she'd just intrigued him with her strength, her beauty, her self-reliance. It probably wouldn't have gone any further than that, had they not been thrown together by their mutual concern for Quinn and the company.

All right, he was interested in her. But all his instincts told him it would be a mistake to attempt anything more than friendship with Julianna. They already had a history, and no matter how much she might say she'd forgotten about it, that history had to be a painful, or at least embarrassing, one as far as she was concerned.

And he'd be leaving. Sooner or later he'd go back on active duty, whether he was cleared to fly or not. He'd leave Colorado Springs, and he didn't intend to leave any broken hearts behind him.

So he and Juli were destined to be friends—that was all. Just friends.

They cleared the belt of trees and came out into an open grassy space. On one side the mountain loomed, painted sharply against a sky that was streaked now with muted tones of red and orange.

On the other side of the level space, the valley dipped. The road they'd come up was a pale ribbon, twisting back and forth in a series of S turns. The area between mountain and valley was a kind of natural amphitheatre, thronged now with people, some in casual Western dress, many in Native American attire.

He inhaled. "Is that sausage I smell?"

"If you're hungry, you can find just about anything you want to eat, of every ethnic variety." She smiled, nodding toward the rows of stalls that had become a temporary marketplace.

"Maybe I'll have something later. Mom practically force-fed me supper."

"That's a sign of love. Like my grandmother and her gnocchi."

"I know." He patted his stomach. "I just don't want to be loved so much I can't fit into my clothes."

She shot a sideways glance at him. "I don't think you need to worry." Then, as if regretting saying something that might be interpreted as a compliment, she glanced at her watch. "We have time before the dances start. Let's find my grandmother's stall."

She started purposefully down a row of stalls. He hurried to keep up with her.

"Does she have a food stand?"

Her eyebrows lifted. "My grandmother is Leona Red Feather."

Clearly he'd goofed. He stepped around a trio of youngsters in Native dress, playing some sort of game in the middle of the aisle. One tot, a little girl who couldn't have been more than three or four, stared gravely from beneath a blue-and-yellow headband adorned with feathers. He smiled at her before turning back to Juli.

"I'm sorry. I guess that name should mean something to me, but it doesn't." He had a feeling he'd just fallen a little in Juli's estimation.

"I suppose you wouldn't know her name unless you were interested in jewelry. My grandmother is one of the finest makers of Zuni silver jewelry." She nodded, turned to a booth. "As you'll see."

"Juli!" The woman behind the counter must be Juli's grandmother, but she had a slim, erect figure and a composed, smiling face. Not a trace of gray showed in her black hair. "You came."

"I said I'd be here." Juli leaned across the counter to hug her. "Grandmother, this is my friend, Kenneth Vance."

Her friend. Well, that was what he'd just told himself he wanted, wasn't it?

He extended his hand and found himself scrutinized by a pair of sharp black eyes. While Juli's grandfather had an open, ebullient manner that seemed to embrace the world, her grandmother measured him gravely.

Not just him. He suspected that if anyone or anything got in her way or condescended to her, she would simply walk past it, head held high. Juli had acquired that dignity of hers honestly.

"It's a pleasure to meet you, Mrs. Red Feather. I met your husband at the construction company office a while back."

"Yes, he told me." The dark eyes still withheld judgment. "And now you've come to see him dance."

"He invited me, and I wanted to come. I'm afraid he pushed Juli into bringing me, though."

She glanced at her granddaughter, love softening her gaze. "Our Juli does as she pleases. She wouldn't have brought you if she hadn't wanted to."

Juli looked slightly flustered—not an expression he'd seen on her face before. "I was just telling him about your work," she said, changing the subject. "I think he'd like to see some examples."

Her grandmother nodded slightly and turned away from them. When she turned back, it was to set a tray on the counter. She flipped off the covering cloth.

Ken's breath caught. He might not know much about jewelry, but he knew beautiful artistry when he saw it. Against a dark woven cloth, earrings and pins of intricately worked silver, set with turquoise, jet and coral, glowed like a pirate's treasure.

"These are beautiful." He looked at Juli's grandmother with increased respect. "You're an artist, not a craftsperson."

She bowed her head gently, a queen accepting her due. "A lapidary, perhaps. Our Juli is the artist of the family."

"Juli?" He raised his eyebrows at her. "Have you been hiding your talent from us?"

She shook her head, and he thought she was embarrassed.

"I don't know how my grandmother can say that. I enjoy painting, but my work is nothing like hers." She bent over the tray, perhaps to hide her face. "Look at the intricate work on this pin." She touched a pin with small stones, each set in its delicate silver bezel. "This style of setting is called needlework."

"You have to help me choose something for Holly." He looked at Juli's grandmother. "Holly is my twin sister. She's expecting a baby, and she's been having a difficult time. A gift of your beautiful work would cheer her up."

"I know—your twin is our Juli's friend." She touched a row of silver bracelets ornamented with designs and turquoise. "Perhaps one of these would please her."

He picked one up. The intricate design seemed to be either a snake or a lightning strike, or maybe a combination of the two. "This is very—"

"Not that one!" Juli's voice was sharp, her eyes wide and haunted. "Don't give that to Holly."

"Juli—" Her grandmother began.

Juli shook her head. She swallowed, her throat working, and attempted a smile. It wasn't very successful. "I'm sorry. Grandmother will help you choose. I think I need something cold to drink."

She turned away and disappeared into the crowd before he could find a word to say.

"I'm the one who's sorry," he said. He put the silver bracelet down gently. "I've done something wrong, but I don't know what."

"It's nothing," Juli's grandmother said smoothly. "If you like the worked silver, why not this hummingbird bracelet? The hummingbird is a symbol for joy and thankfulness. That would be good for a pregnant woman, I think."

The hummingbird was set with the tiniest fragments of colored stones in work so intricate he couldn't begin to imagine how difficult it was. "She'll love it." He reached for his wallet.

"I'll put it in a box for you." She smiled, removing the tiny price tag. "And of course there's a fifteen percent discount for being Juli's friend."

"You don't need to do that." Admittedly the bracelet was expensive, but it was nothing he couldn't afford for the sake of making Holly smile.

"I want to." Her simple courtesy made it impossible to argue. She slipped the bracelet into a box and wrapped the box in tissue paper, her hands moving deftly.

He tried to forget it, but Juli's reaction to the first bracelet haunted him. "You said the hummingbird was a symbol of joy and thankfulness. What does the snake symbolize?"

Her serene expression didn't change, but she hesitated. "The old ones saw a relationship between the strike of lightning and the strike of a snake, so the two symbols are linked. Usually the snake stands for energy and change."

There didn't seem anything in that to cause Juli's reaction. "Why did Juli react so strongly to that bracelet, then?"

She eyed him for a moment, and he could feel her weighing whether or not to tell him. Finally she sighed, looking down at her hands, tying a bow on the small package.

"Juli's mother, my daughter—she always wore a bracelet with the zigzag symbol of the snake. Juli was very young when her mother died—somehow she always associated that symbol with her mother's death."

There was more to it than that. He could sense it. For some reason he couldn't understand, he had to know.

"How did Juli's mother die?"

Her fingers stilled on the package—strong, capable hands lax for an instant. Would she tell him? Only if she chose to, and if she did, it would mean something about her measure of him as a person.

After a long moment, she spoke. "She went out alone in a storm, and her car had a flat. She was trying to change a tire when lightning struck. She was killed instantly."

"We'd better get over to the arena if we're going to see the Grand Entry."

Julianna hadn't really been thirsty, but getting the cup of iced tea had given her time to regroup. Now she could smile at Ken in what she hoped was a natural manner.

"Sure thing." Ken turned away from the booth, sliding the small package into his pocket. "Thank you, Mrs. Red Feather. I hope we'll meet again."

"We will." Grandmother gave them both that enigmatic smile that never failed to nettle Julianna.

Well, if her grandmother was matchmaking, she'd be doomed to failure, just as Holly was. Ken wasn't interested in anything other than getting back to his interrupted life.

"Your grandmother is an impressive woman," he said. "And I don't just mean as an artist. She looks like someone to reckon with."

She nodded. He'd assessed her grandmother accurately after a brief meeting. "In Pueblo culture, women have always held a high position and had considerable independence. They often pass on their names, their property, their position, to the children."

"A very enlightened attitude—it's easy to see where you get your independence." He smiled. "A quality I admire, by the way."

Unsure how to respond to that, she hastened her steps. Ken kept pace with her. The arena wasn't really that—just an open circular space where the grass was tamped down. The watchers had already begun to gather in a loose group around the area, listening to the drums and talking in soft voices. Although it wasn't dark yet, torches had been lit around the perimeter.

"Do you want to go across to—"

She caught Ken before he had a chance to step into the arena. "Not that way." She started around the crowd, nodding to people she knew.

Ken stayed on her heels, as close as Angel would. "Obviously I almost made my first blunder. What was it?"

"I guess I didn't do a very good job of orienting you." She'd been too prickly, just because it was Ken. Had any other friend been with her, she wouldn't have hesitated to explain the traditions to him or her. "The arena is considered—well, it's sacred in the sense of being set apart from ordinary use. No one goes into the arena except under the direction of the master of ceremonies."

He took her hand, swinging it lightly between them as they walked. "Thanks for saving me from looking ignorant, then."

Too aware of the warmth of his hand on hers, she found a place with a good view of the entry to the arena. More people greeted her, good-naturedly pushing her and Ken to the front when they saw she had brought a guest.

"Looks as if you know everyone here."

"I should. Grandfather started bringing me when I was just a baby." A spurt of affection went through her. These were her people, gathered to celebrate their traditions in a way that went back perhaps thousands of years.

"Are they all Zuni, like your family?"

She hadn't realized he remembered which Pueblo her family belonged to. "No. Once, maybe, that would have been true, but now many powwows are like this one—All Nations. You'll see a lot of different types of dances and different regalia. What Grandfather wears is traditional Zuni."

Ken smiled. "He's a pretty impressive person. I'm looking forward to seeing him dance." He paused, as if there was something he wanted to say.

"What?" She nudged him with her elbow. "You can ask anything about the powwow."

His eyebrow lifted. "Even if it's personal?"

"Try me."

"I assume you wouldn't be coming to Bible study unless you're a Christian. So how do the Native American traditions fit into that?"

It was a fair question, and coming from anyone else, she wouldn't hesitate to answer. For some reason, the fact that it came from Ken seemed to raise her hackles a bit.

She tried to keep her tone neutral. "There was a time when the dances were considered—well, pagan, I guess you'd say. Many Christian Native Americans feared it was wrong to participate, and some outsiders even tried to stop the dances."

"I take it they didn't succeed."

Her smile flickered. "For once, the courts came down on our side. My grandfather is probably the most devout Christian I know, and he says participating in the dances is a way of preserving our heritage, not a matter of religion. That's probably true of most of the people here. We find it possible to be Christians without giving up our identity as a people."

"You explain it very well, Juli." The corners of his eyes crinkled. "Even to an outsider like me."

The words startled her. She was so used to seeing herself as the outsider and Ken as the ultimate insider. He'd given her another way of looking at their roles.

The drums, which had been silent, began their insistent beat again, and her pulse seemed to throb in time with them. The crowd turned as one toward the entry space that had been left in the circle. Footsteps in time with the drums, the jingle of small bells, the rustle of expectancy in the crowd—all this announced the entry of the dancers.

She put her hand on Ken's arm, nodding toward the entry. Did he feel any of what she did—the sense that here, under the darkening sky, high above their ordinary lives, they were in touch with the divine? She looked toward the mountain, looming above them in pristine majesty.

"I will lift up mine eyes unto the hills; from whence cometh my help. My help comes from the Lord, the Maker of Heaven and Earth."

A splash of color, the ripple of flags, the murmur of the crowd, and the dancers entered the arena, feet moving on the rough ground in time to the drums.

"Flag bearers come first," she murmured to Ken. "The head dancers will be next—that's where you'll see Grandfather."

He nodded, smiling, and clasped her hand again. His was warm and strong, and a frisson of tenderness went through her. If Ken were ever ready to love, if he found the right woman, he would have so much to offer.

It wouldn't be her. She knew that. But for the moment she didn't ask anything more than to stand here next to him, holding hands, sharing something that was precious to her. Whether Ken knew it or not, this evening was one she'd remember for a long time.

The dances proceeded through their progression. Children's groups, men, women—all had their part. The Hopi family next to them offered a blanket, and she sat next to Ken, aware of the warmth that emanated from him as the evening grew cooler. Once in a while he asked a question or she explained a dance, but for the most part they were quiet, watching. Contented.

Or at least, she had been contented. A shiver went through her suddenly, and the hair on the back of her neck rose like Angel's when she sensed something wrong.

"What is it? Are you cold?" Ken put his arm around her shoulders, and she had to resist the longing to lean into his strength.

"No, it's not that." She rubbed the back of her neck, as if she could rub away the feeling. "I just felt as if someone were watching me. Watching us."

He studied her face, smiling a little. "They probably are. Probably wondering what bright, accomplished

Julianna Red Feather is doing here with a washed up pilot."

"Not that kind of feeling."

How could she explain that sense of inimical eyes fixed on them? She shivered again. She was imagining things, wasn't she? But she'd learned, during her years of search-and-rescue, to trust her instincts, and those instincts told her this was no idle curiosity.

She stretched and turned, casually scanning the crowd behind them. No one seemed to be watching them. No face stood out as not belonging there. Still, she couldn't seem to shake off the feeling.

"Okay?" The gaze he turned on her was troubled.

She shrugged, trying to smile. "I guess. The men's dances are about over. Maybe we ought to greet Grandfather and then head back down the mountain."

"If that's what you want."

She nodded. She was being silly, she supposed, but—

Instinct. The word echoed in her mind. She ought to trust her instinct.

It didn't take more than a few minutes to find Grandfather in the crowd. He was flushed with exertion and the success of his dance, and clearly delighted that they'd come.

"Kenneth." He pumped Ken's hand. "So what do you think of your first powwow?"

"Impressive, very impressive. And Julianna was right—you were the best."

"I told you so." Julianna stretched on tiptoe to kiss her grandfather's leathery cheek, careful not to touch the intricate turquoise beadwork that trimmed his black blouse. "You'll have to retire sometime, just to give some of the younger men a chance to shine."

"Did you introduce Ken to your grandmother?"

"Of course." She kept her smile in place with an effort, remembering her foolish weakness. "He even bought a bracelet for Holly."

"It's a work of art," Ken said. "I'm ashamed to admit that all this was going on and I hadn't even noticed."

"Well, now you know." Grandfather patted his shoulder. "And you'll come back again. You're always welcome."

"I'll see you tomorrow." Julianna gave her grandfather a quick hug. "We're heading back now."

"Drive carefully." Grandfather kissed her cheek, and then he turned away with a last nod as one of the other dancers came up to speak to him.

Her feet found the path back to the parking area, even in the dark. Ken, close behind her, didn't speak until they'd reached the car.

"I meant what I said to your grandfather, you know." He unlocked the door. "It embarrasses me that this rich cultural tradition is going on in our midst and I never noticed."

"That's not so unusual," she said, sliding into the passenger's side. "Things have started to change now, but for a long time, we preferred to keep our traditions quiet. Maybe it was a way of ensuring that they didn't slip away."

"I can understand that." He pulled out of the lot. "But I'm glad you agreed to bring me tonight, Juli. It's an evening I won't forget."

Odd, his echoing what she'd been thinking, too. But their reasons were different. Her mind had been on Ken, while his was preoccupied with the cultural tradition he'd met tonight.

"Turn right out of the park entrance." She hesitated, smiling. "I don't mean to be a backseat driver. I just thought you might not remember these mountain roads after being away for so long."

"It's coming back to me."

The road swept downhill almost immediately, and the darkness was complete once they'd left the park behind. The peak loomed to their left, a darker shadow against the darkening sky.

The headlights picked up the S-shaped warning sign for the hairpin curves that were coming up, and a shiver went through her at its similarity to the snake symbol. She suppressed it angrily.

How could she have betrayed her feelings so clearly, and in front of Ken, of all people? If he knew what was behind her reaction, he'd think her ridiculously superstitious.

She wasn't. She just didn't want Holly wearing something she associated with her mother's death. That wasn't unreasonable, was it?

Ken's capable hands moved on the steering wheel as they approached the first curve. He put his foot lightly on the brake pedal to slow the car.

Nothing happened. She saw his face tense, sensed his grip tighten as he pressed harder.

Nothing. They hurtled down the dark mountain, gathering speed.

She grabbed the arm rest, gripping tightly. "What is it? What's happening?"

Ken swerved, tires screaming. "The brakes are gone. Hold on."

EIGHT

Ken pumped the brakes, his mind and body totally focused on the task at hand. Block everything else out—that was what you did when you faced an emergency.

Pump the brakes. Nothing. The pedal went straight to the floor, and another S curve was coming up, with its sheer drop-off to the right, to the valley floor.

The emergency brake—but it went straight to the floor, too.

He hugged the left side as if the mountain would protect them, yanking the shift into low, praying nothing would come barreling toward them around the curve. He fought the wheel, hearing the tires shriek as they clung to the road.

Out of the curve, but they were picking up speed, hurtling down the mountain at a terrifying rate. *Concentrate, think what else might work, don't think about anything else. Don't think about Julianna, clinging to the armrest, her other hand braced against the dash. Letting anything else in was a useless distraction.*

But he heard, through the roaring in his ears, the soft murmur of her voice. Praying.

Another curve—how many were there before the road straightened out to that long level stretch before it dipped down for the last time?

Too many. They'd never make it.

Never make it. For an instant he was back in the cockpit, screaming through the air, knowing he was hit, he was going down—

No. That was then, this was now. Julianna's life depended on his cool head.

He'd gone too far to the right. The car scraped the guardrail, metal shrieking, slowing slightly. He pulled to the left, fighting the wheel.

"I'm going to steer onto the left berm. Hold on."

"Right." She sounded remarkably calm.

Better to risk running into the side of the mountain than off the edge. The scraggly bushes that overgrew the berm screamed along the driver's side door, slowing them, giving him hope. If he could slow a bit more, find a sloping bank, they might yet get out of this in one piece.

His luck, if he had any, ran out. The front wheel hit a rain-washed gully along the side of the road, grinding them to a jarring halt. With a muffled explosion the airbags deployed, thrusting him back against the seat. His head spun, and for an instant he couldn't breathe.

Julianna—he gasped for breath, fighting his way out of the entangling folds of the airbag.

"Juli! Are you all right?" He grasped for her, his vision blurring in the uptilted glare of their headlights.

Her hand clasped his, warm and strong. "I'm okay."

Incredibly, she managed a shaky laugh. "I just can't seem to get out of the seatbelt."

"Easy. Are you sure you're okay?" His vision seemed to clear. He reached for the dome light, switching it on. In the dim glow Juli smiled at him from behind the muffling folds of the airbag.

"Fine. You?"

"In one piece, surprisingly enough." He unbuckled his seatbelt and slid over, pushing the airbag out of the way. He couldn't open his door—it had smacked against the bank.

Fumbling, he found the buckle of her seatbelt and undid it. Juli, released, slid against him.

"Sorry." Her breath was soft against his cheek. "We seem to have landed on a slant."

"We're lucky we didn't land smashed into a million pieces at the foot of the mountain," he growled. His arms went around her without thought, and he pulled her even closer. "You could have been killed. I shouldn't—"

Her fingers covered his lips. "I'm sure you're about to find some way to blame yourself for this, but don't even try. You knew what to do. If I'd been driving, I wouldn't have made it past that first S curve."

Her voice shook a little on the words, and he had a sudden vision of what that S curve looked like to her.

"Juli—"

He just wanted to reassure her, to comfort her. Without thought, his lips found hers, tentatively at first, and then more surely as her arms went around him and her lips softened under his.

Tenderness flowed through him. She was so sweet,

so caring, and he wanted to hold her close and kiss her
until they'd both forgotten where they were and why.

His breath caught, and he pulled back. He shouldn't
be doing this.

Juli's face was scant inches from his. Her eyes had
a dazed look, maybe from the shock of the accident,
maybe from the kiss.

"Sorry." He brushed a loose strand of hair back from
her face, her skin smooth and warm to his touch. "I
guess I got a little carried away."

"It's all right." Her voice was husky, and she made
no effort to pull away from him. "Seemed like a good
idea to me, too."

"In that case—"

A shaft of light hit them, illuminating the inside of
the car like a spotlight. He pulled away, holding up one
hand to shield his eyes.

Both doors of a pickup truck flew open, and two
people started toward them, dark figures against the light.
He tensed. Good Samaritans, probably, but if not—

"You folks okay?" The man scrambled along the
bank to shine the beam of a flashlight in at the driver's
side window. Pueblo, Ken guessed the man was,
wearing a loose, dark shirt with a headband tied around
his forehead. His face was creased with concern. The
second person, smaller and slighter, was back there in
the shadows.

"We're okay, but we're going to need some help to
get out of here."

"Hold tight. We'll get you both out the passenger

side." The flashlight flickered to that seat. "Juli! I didn't know it was you. You okay?"

"I'm fine, Dan." Juli struggled to put another inch of space between them. "Ken, this is Dan Nieto." Her voice seemed to change slightly. "He's Jay's father."

Jay appeared behind his father, his expression scared as he set to work getting them out of the car. So Jay had been at the powwow. He filed that away to consider later. He couldn't talk to Juli, because other cars began pulling up behind them as people, leaving the powwow, realized what had happened.

Harvey Red Feather rushed up to enfold Juli in his arms. "Juli, are you all right?"

She must be getting tired of answering that question, but she snuggled into her grandfather's arms, nodding. Ken couldn't suppress a pang of what had to be envy. A few minutes ago she'd been in his arms.

"I'm sorry, sir." He met the man's gaze over Juli's bent head. "I didn't take very good care of her."

"Not your fault." Juli's grandfather studied the car, frowning. "Looks like you did a pretty fair job of landing that thing. A rental, isn't it?"

He nodded. "I hate to think what my insurance company is going to say."

"The brakes went?"

"Completely gone, as well as the emergency brake."

Harvey seemed to hold Juli a little tighter. "That's odd."

"Yes." He sounded grim. Well, he felt grim. Either someone at the rental company was guilty of gross carelessness, or else...

Or else it hadn't been an accident. His mind flashed

back to Juli's nervousness, her sense that they were being watched. She would hate him for thinking it, but he very much wondered whether Jay Nieto had been under his father's eyes the entire time he was at the powwow.

It was late—too late to be going down the rickety steps into the tunnel, but she didn't exactly have a choice. When he summoned her, she had to come.

For now. Eventually that would change, but for the time being, she'd play her role.

He waited for her in the damp room, pacing back and forth, his whipcord-lean body tense with anger. She approached cautiously.

"What's wrong?"

He whirled on her. "I've just heard. That idiot O'Brien hired loused it up. Kenneth Vance survived again, without a scratch on him."

"Yes, I heard." She kept her voice low and even. Sometimes she could calm him. Always he teetered on the brink of losing control. "It was always a chance. It's not easy to make something look like an accident and be sure of fatal results."

"Easy?" His face twisted. "I'm paying for results. I don't care how easy or hard it is. I want him dead."

She took a cautious breath. "You said you wanted to keep them off-balance. Your orders were only to act directly against him if it could be made to look like an accident."

His fist clenched, but she didn't think he was so far gone that he'd strike her. He might threaten, but he depended upon her. Still, there was always the chance that his mania would outweigh everything else.

"Look, my darling." She made her tone soft, caressing. "We'll get all your enemies. We will. But right now we should be concentrating on the latest shipment."

"Do you think I cannot do both?"

"No, of course not." Dealing with him was walking a tightrope. "But you haven't fully recovered your strength yet. You must give yourself time. Time, and they will fall into your hands like a ripe plum."

"Always you speak sense, *querida*." He stepped closer, and she forced herself not to cringe when his hand wrapped around her throat.

"That is my job, isn't it?"

"That, and other things." He drew her closer. "I understand that woman, Julianna, was with him again tonight. Are they becoming involved?"

"Kenneth Vance, with her? Nonsense. The Vances of this world don't become involved with people like her."

His laugh rasped. "I've seen her. Any man would be interested."

"I don't think—"

His grip tightened, his face thrusting toward hers like a snake. "You're interested in him yourself, aren't you?"

"Of course not." Fear curled in her stomach, but she wouldn't let it have sway over her. "I need no one but you, my darling."

His fingers pressed. For an instant her head swam, the dark cavern turning blood red. Then he released her.

"As long as you remember that." He turned away,

pacing the width of the small room as if it were a cage. Or a cell. "This Julianna—tell O'Brien. She is a target as well. Anyone who aids my enemy is my enemy. And hurting her will hurt Kenneth Vance."

"I'll tell him." Anything to calm him down. Besides, what did she care if Julianna Red Feather suffered?

"Good. Good." He slumped into a chair, his manic energy seeming exhausted. She wondered, not for the first time, if he'd been sampling his own wares.

"I'll go and call O'Brien, then."

He nodded, lowering his head to rest on his arms. "All my enemies," he murmured. "All will be punished."

She backed away cautiously. Escalante was becoming a liability. Still, as long as the money poured in, she would bide her time. When she struck, she wanted to be sure she had enough to spend the rest of her life in anonymous luxury.

She mounted the stairs and pressed the latch that opened the door. It was ironic, and she enjoyed irony. On this side of the door she was the second in command to a drug lord. Step through, close the door, and she was in her elegant office. Dahlia Sainsbury, curator of the Impressionist Museum, working late as she often did.

In fact, she was neither of those personas, but no one would know the truth until it was too late.

It was not the first time Julianna had come into the office late and groggy from lack of sleep, but she certainly hoped it was the last. Her grandfather had insisted on driving her home the previous night, leaving Ken waiting with the wrecked rental car for the tow truck.

Maybe it was just as well that she hadn't had another opportunity to talk with Ken. While he'd nodded and smiled at everyone who said what an unfortunate accident it was, she'd sensed the aura of suspicion that emanated from him. Sensed it, and known she was too shaken to deal with it.

In fact, she still wasn't ready to cope. She could only hope Ken had decided that the late night gave him a good excuse to sleep in this morning.

The long, low office building nestled against the red barn that housed the design and cabinetry divisions like a chick against a mother hen. She had her key out as she approached the door, but it was already unlocked. Clearly she hadn't succeeded in beating everyone here.

Quinn swung from the coffeemaker when she entered, looking dismayed. "Julianna. What are you doing here? I heard about the accident. You don't look fit to be out of bed."

She grimaced. "Since I wasn't injured, that's really not much of a compliment."

He crossed the office and gave her a quick hug. "You know what I mean. You look exhausted, and it's no wonder. What does that idiot friend of mine mean by smashing you up against a mountainside?"

"Your idiot friend got smashed, too, remember?"

Her heartbeat accelerated at the sound of Ken's voice, and she turned slowly to see him standing in the doorway.

"Hey, I figure a tough Air Force pilot like you

wouldn't be bothered by a little thing like that." Quinn studied his friend's face. "Tell you the truth, you don't look so good either."

"I always look like this after a hair-raising escape from death, ol' buddy." Ken crossed the office to lean against the desk next to her. "Why don't you send Juli home?"

"That's what I was trying to do before you so rudely interrupted. For that matter, you go home, too. Believe it or not, Montgomery Construction can get along without the two of you for one day."

"I have no intention of going home," she said firmly. She tossed her bag into her desk drawer and slid into her chair. "Now if you two will just get out of my hair, maybe I can get some work done."

Quinn lifted his hands in despair. "All right, all right. I don't know which of the pair of you is more stubborn. Stay if you're so bent on doing it, but if anyone keels over today, I'm not taking responsibility."

He grabbed his coffee mug and headed into his office, closing the door behind him.

She couldn't look at Ken, not after the way Quinn had insisted on pairing them together. But Quinn hadn't meant anything by it—she knew he hadn't. It was just the memory of that kiss that was clouding her mind, making her see innuendo where there was nothing but friendship.

She would not look at Ken. If she did, her face might give something away.

And it was ridiculous, anyway. She was imagining a bond that didn't exist. Any two people who'd gone through a traumatic ordeal together might have feelings that—

Ken leaned over the desk, touching the bruise on her forehead with a gentle brush of his fingertips that she seemed to feel all the way to her heart.

"I didn't notice this last night. I guess it was too dark. Did you have it checked out?"

"Of course not." She tried to sound impatient, because if she let him see how she really felt their relationship would become impossible. "I've had far worse when I've been deployed on a mission, and believe me, no one gets very excited about a few bruises."

"You weren't out on a dangerous mission. You were just riding down the mountain in my car, and you were nearly killed." His voice was somber, and she knew he was blaming himself again.

"I wasn't, thanks to you. If I didn't say it last night, I'll say it now. Your good driving saved both our lives. If we'd gone over the edge—"

She shouldn't have mentioned that. It made the images too alive in her mind.

"I guess we're matching now." He touched the scar on his forehead.

It was the first time he'd referred to his injury lightly, and she managed a smile in response. "We could get matching outfits."

"Somehow I don't think so." But he was still smiling, and she felt as if she'd accomplished her good deed for the day in wiping the worry from his eyes.

He crossed to the coffeemaker and poured out a mug. "Do you want some of this? Quinn makes it strong enough to hold the spoon upright."

"That sounds like just what I need this morning."

He poured a second mug and brought it to her. "Bad dreams?"

She shrugged. "I get them sometimes. It doesn't necessarily have anything to do with the accident."

"If it was an accident," he muttered.

"What do you mean?" She set the mug down, standing to face him. "If there's more to it than brake failure, I have a right to know that."

"The brakes failed all right. And the emergency brakes. The chances of that happening on a fairly new rental car are pretty slim, don't you think?"

"I don't know." She didn't want to think about it. She wanted to bury her head in a pillow and forget.

Ken's face was grim. "I do. So I went back to the garage and waited for the mechanic. I made sure he went over that car with a fine-tooth comb."

She wouldn't be a coward about it. "What did he find?"

"The brake lines had been cut. That didn't happen by accident, Juli. It happened while the car was parked at the powwow."

Even while she was shaking her head, she knew he was telling her the truth. She'd sensed it, hadn't she? Her instincts had told her that someone was watching them, wishing them ill.

"You think it was Jay, don't you?"

"He was there."

Her anger flared. "So were several hundred other people. It could have been anyone."

"I know that." He shook his head impatiently and then grabbed her hands. "Juli—"

He stopped, looking at her. That meant that he felt it, too—that irrational surge of attraction between them.

His hard grip gentled, until it was almost a caress. "And this complicates matters."

"What do you mean?" She had to pretend she didn't know.

"This." His fingers moved gently across the palms of her hands. "Us." He shook his head. "I'm not a safe person to be around. Bad luck seems to be following me."

She took a breath, trying to think past the thrumming of her nerves in response to his touch. "I don't believe in luck, good or bad."

"Actually I don't either. But I'm still not going to expose you to it, whatever it is."

She met his eyes. "If you're thinking that Jay cut those brake lines—"

"Actually, I'm not. At least, not on his own."

"I don't understand."

He shook his head. "I'm not sure what's going on, but I am sure that wasn't a simple act of vandalism."

A shudder went through her. If Ken's reactions had been a fraction of a second slower they'd both have been dead.

"Whoever did it had to know we'd be headed back down the mountain after the powwow." The S curve sign seemed to flash in her mind like a warning.

"Right. This isn't in the same ballpark as putting sugar in gas tanks and painting on walls."

"You should tell Quinn. And your cousin." The police would come into it. They'd have to.

"Right. I will." His hands moved absently on hers, as if he'd forgotten he still held them. "Look, Juli, so far everything has been directed at the Vances and the Montgomerys, but you were with me last night."

"I don't think that matters. Really—"

The pressure of his hands cut off her words. "Maybe it's nothing, but I'd feel a lot better if I knew you were being careful. Keep Angel with you when you can, all right? She'd scare any bad guys off in a hurry."

"She would, wouldn't she?" She smiled, touched by the concern and caring in his voice. "I'll be careful, but I think you're right. This isn't aimed at me."

"Well." He straightened, letting go of her hands. "I guess I'd better go tell Quinn the bad news."

She nodded, wishing she didn't feel so reluctant to let him go. "And I'd better get to work. Montgomery Construction isn't paying me to sit around."

She flipped on the computer, watching him walk toward Quinn's office door while she waited for it to boot up. It probably would make a lot more sense to send Angel along with him as a watchdog, but she didn't suppose Ken would agree to that.

She turned to the computer and stumbled back a step, the chair clattering, a cry choked in her throat. She stared, heart pounding, dimly aware of Ken reaching her, grasping her shoulders.

She couldn't tear her gaze from the screen. Her usual blue desktop was gone. Instead, the screen glared with a red symbol on a black background—the zigzag line that struck at her heart like lightning.

NINE

Quinn had finally insisted she take the rest of the day off, and Julianna had to admit he'd been right. She'd taken Angel out to Palmer Park and run them both until she'd been physically exhausted enough to sleep.

She'd come in all the earlier this morning, rested and ready to put in some extra time to make up for having been off the previous day. Quinn had said he'd have an expert go over her computer for any clue to how the hacker had gained access and to look for any other problems, but it seemed to her that she was far more likely to spot something wrong than a stranger would.

She'd said once to Ken that she remembered figures, and she wasn't sure he'd believed or understood. She couldn't explain it herself—that was just the kind of mind she had. If anyone had tampered with any of the financial reports on her computer, she'd know it.

A uniformed guard stepped out in front of the car as she approached the gate. Apparently Quinn was taking the stepped-up security he'd talked about seriously.

"'Morning, miss." The elderly man touched his hat brim as he approached her car window. Lou Davis didn't look especially threatening, but he seemed to be taking his new responsibilities seriously. "You're here early."

"I thought I'd get in some extra time at the office."

His brow wrinkled. "Well, miss, that's a bit of a problem. See, they changed all the locks on the offices yesterday, and I can't leave the gate to let you in."

So much for getting an early start. She might as well have had that second cup of coffee. "Can't you just give me the key?"

"Sorry. Mr. Quinn, he gave strict orders not to give my key to anybody."

"But I'm the office manager."

"Sorry," he repeated.

Her stomach churned. She'd thought she was a trusted member of the team. Obviously she'd been wrong. "How am I supposed to get in, then?"

"Mr. Vance came in about half an hour ago. I guess he could let you in."

"Fine." She threw the car into drive, mentally rehearsing just what she'd say to Ken about locking her out of her own office. "I'll find him."

Lou nodded, stepping back to open the gate. She smiled at him as she drove through. It wasn't right to be short with Lou. He was just doing his job.

Ken was another story. He had to have been in on this decision with Quinn.

She parked and checked the office. Locked and dark. Where was Ken? If she'd brought Angel with her, as he'd suggested, she could have found him in minutes. As it was—

A movement in the debris area caught her eye, and she started toward it. That was Ken, all right. Wearing shorts and a T-shirt, he appeared to be running around the debris field.

She frowned as she approached. He was driving himself pretty hard. She'd think, with an eye injury, that pounding along an improvised running track wasn't the best way of exercising.

She slowed as she approached him. He hadn't noticed her. His face was set, his shirt wet with perspiration. Maybe she should wait.

But he seemed to be slowing. He stopped at the ladder they'd left in place after the last training session, bending over, breathing hard, and she knew instinctively he wouldn't want her to see him showing any sign of weakness.

He straightened, looking up the ladder, and then he began to climb. She bit her lip. That definitely looked as if he were pushing too hard. Still, interfering would probably just encourage him to do more out of sheer contrariness.

Just as she started to turn away, Ken reached the top of the ladder and stepped out onto the plank. Okay, that did it. She started toward him. If he didn't have enough sense to know that was dangerous, she'd have to interfere.

She hadn't gone more than a few steps when Ken stopped, frozen in place, balancing on the plank a good ten feet in the air. Her breath caught. He put his hand to his head, his eyes seeming to lose focus.

Heedless of upsetting or embarrassing him, she darted forward, reaching him just as he toppled from the plank. She dived, her arms closing around him to break his fall, and they both tumbled into the stack of cardboard boxes under the plank.

"Are you all right?" She fought her way free of the boxes, catching her breath. "Ken?"

He shoved himself to his feet and planted his fists on his hips. "Why were you spying on me?"

She got up slowly, instinct telling her not to snap back at him. She suspected his frustration was with himself, not her, and the only thing she could do was try to take the situation lightly.

"Hey, take it easy. I won't tell your mother on you. I promise."

For an instant his reaction hung in the balance. Then he flushed. "Sorry," he muttered. "I didn't mean to snap."

"I know." She studied his face, wondering what was going through his mind. "Seemed like you were pushing yourself pretty hard." She tried to keep her tone neutral.

"Yeah." He ran his hand through his hair. He was still breathing hard, his chest rising and falling with the effort he'd expended. "I have to get back into shape."

"I'd say you're in pretty good shape already after what you've been through."

He shot her an annoyed look. "Not good enough."

"Not good enough for what?" She was probably pushing her luck, but concern for him drove her.

"Anybody ever tell you you're too persistent?"

She smiled, relieved he didn't flare out at her again. "Funny, I always thought persistence was a good quality."

"Sometimes." He gave her a reluctant smile in return. "Okay, if you must know. I have a physical exam with an Air Force doctor coming up in a couple of weeks. I intend to pass it."

"Pass it—you mean as in get certified to fly again?"

"That's right. It's time I got back to what I was born to do."

A wave of compassion swept over her. Ken was setting himself up for grief. She didn't have the right to speak, but someone had to, and she suspected she was the only one who knew what he had planned. That put the responsibility on her.

Lord, give me the right words.

"Don't you think maybe you're rushing things? It hasn't been that long."

"Long enough." His face set in grim lines. "I can't stay here, wasting my life. I'm ready to go."

He wasn't ready. Anyone who'd seen him fall from the plank could have told him that. There was no way he'd be able to pass the rigorous exam this quickly.

And if he did, somehow, manage to pass? If so, he'd be gone in an instant without a backward glance. A woman would have to be crazy to fall for a man whose heart belonged to the wild blue yonder.

Not that she was doing any such thing, of course.

"Enough about that." Ken shrugged, as if he wanted to shrug off having confided in her. "What are you doing here so early?"

Her initial irritation came rushing back. "Trying to get some extra work done. I wanted to go over the financial records on my computer, but that's a little hard to do since I'm locked out of my own office."

"Locked out?" He seemed to remember. "Oh, right. Quinn had all the locks changed yesterday. Well, he had to. Obviously someone had had access to your computer in spite of all the security."

"And I'm not to be trusted, is that it?" No matter how irrational it was to feel that way, it still rankled.

"Juli, don't be silly." He pulled a set of keys from the pocket of his shorts. "We just decided that the fewer keys were out, the safer we'd be. Come on. I'll let you in."

He stalked off toward the office, not looking back to see if she was coming. It was business as usual for him. And what he'd said made perfect sense.

She just couldn't help the feeling that she was being shut out, the outsider yet again.

Much of the hospital addition was at the bare bones stage inside, even though the exterior walls were up. Ken watched his step as he worked his way around it. The site was a maze, with half constructed walls, the shell of an elevator shaft and plenty of places for someone to hide. Or to get hurt.

He wasn't sure which possibility bothered Quinn the most—the idea that the vandals would strike again or the chance that someone would wander onto the property, get hurt and sue Montgomery Construction. In any event, he'd promised Quinn he'd make one more pass before he left for the day.

With any luck, the construction would go quickly

enough that over the next few days the exterior doors and windows would be lockable. Once that was done, the site would be a lot tougher for a vandal to enter. And according to Quinn, the work would go faster as well.

Ken ducked under a dangling sheet of heavy plastic. This area would be the central rotunda of the addition, and even at this stage, Ken could see the beauty of Quinn's design. This project could assure the continued success of Montgomery Construction, but only if it was finished on time and without any damaging incidents.

He passed on through to what would be the office wing of the physical therapy center. A warren of framed-out rooms provided a fine place for mischief, but he didn't see or hear anything.

He rubbed his forehead, where the dull ache that had been with him since the morning threatened to explode into a full-scale, blinding headache. He couldn't think about that without being reminded of how stupid he'd been with Juli. How could he have accused her of spying on him?

Fortunately, she'd been able to forgive him that, but she'd certainly had something stuck in her craw about that business with the keys. He wasn't sure what had been bugging her, and he hadn't felt able to ask.

That was a constant motif, it seemed, with him and Juli. He couldn't dig too deeply, because that would imply a relationship that he wasn't willing to have. Yet he couldn't deny the attraction he felt for her, or the longing he had to understand what inner turmoil hid beneath the strong front she showed to the world.

A sharp clatter, somewhere behind him, had him

spinning around, pulses racing. He moved softly back the way he'd come, senses alert for any sound.

Nothing. The building lay so still around him that only the muted traffic noises from the street intruded.

But there had been something—he was sure of it. He stood in the rotunda, looking up, listening. No sound broke the silence. It was fruitless for one person to play hide and seek through the construction—there were too many places to hide.

He glanced at his watch. The night watchmen would be arriving soon. He'd wait for them outside and tell them to do a thorough patrol first thing.

He walked out the wooden plank to the sidewalk, frowning, reminded of his foolhardiness in trying to walk that two-by-four that morning. What had he been thinking? Even the dogs had difficulty with that one.

He stepped onto the walk and stopped, eyes narrowing at the sight of the boy who stood, leaning against the construction fence. "Jay. What are you doing here?"

Jay shrugged, his thin face reserved. "I went over to the office to see if Juli was all right after the accident, but she'd already left. Just thought I'd come over here and see you instead."

"How did you know I was here?" His voice was too sharp. Going full tilt at the boy would only raise his defenses.

"That old guy on the gate told me."

The boy looked as if he were on the verge of lashing out. He'd better mend fences with the kid if he wanted any information from him.

"Oh, sure," he said easily. "Well, far as I know, Juli's

okay. She bumped her head, but you know Juli. She won't admit anything's wrong, even if it is."

"Yeah." Jay's smile flashed. "She's pretty tough, isn't she?"

"She sure is. I'll tell you though, we were glad to see you and your dad turn up when you did. We appreciated the help."

"It wasn't anything."

"Did you enjoy the powwow?"

Jay shrugged again, reverting to the bored look teenagers seemed to do so well. "It was okay. My dad makes me go. He wants me to dance, but I dunno about that."

"That was my first powwow." How could he get out the question he needed to ask? "I guess you know Juli and her family pretty well, don't you?"

"Pretty well. My dad and her grandpa and grandma go way back."

"Her grandmother showed me the jewelry she makes, with the Zuni designs."

He was edging closer to the question that had given him such a bad feeling. How had they—whoever *they* were—known that the lightning symbol would spook Juli so badly? Quinn had suggested coincidence, but he didn't believe in a coincidence that was so on target.

"Yeah, it's pretty nice, I guess. Lots of people on the pueblo make jewelry like that." The boy was tiring of the subject, starting to edge away.

"Do you know any particular symbols Juli likes? Or doesn't like? I was thinking of getting her something." That sounded pretty feeble, even to him.

Jay pulled back. "How would I know something like that?" Suspicion edged his tone.

Maybe it was time to stop trying to be clever with the kid. "Somebody left a Zuni symbol in the office for Juli to find. One that upset her. I want to know—"

"You think it was me. Just because it was Zuni, you figure I had to be to blame." The boy's face paled, his fists clenched.

"I didn't say that."

"That's what you meant. I know. You figure I can't be trusted. Fine. I don't hang around where I'm not wanted."

With a lightning move, Jay whirled and ran off down the street.

He watched the slight figure disappear around the corner. He'd like to follow, but he had to wait for the night watchmen to get here. And following the kid probably wouldn't do any good, anyway. Ken was now the last person Jay would want to talk to.

One thing was certain. While he wasn't looking forward to confessing what he'd done, he'd better run over to Juli's and let her know what had happened. If anyone could get through to Jay, she could.

But he didn't look forward to the tongue-lashing that was probably in store for him.

Julianna leaned away from the canvas, suddenly aware of the kink in her back. She glanced at her watch, appalled at how late it was getting. She'd been painting since she got home from work, totally absorbed in her creation, unaware of the passage of time.

She didn't need to look at the painting to know what

it was. She'd been caught in quicksand with her painting for months, constantly re-creating variations of the same scene: The storm.

Putting her brush down, she rubbed her back. A psychiatrist would probably have a field day with her paintings—not that she intended for anyone ever to see them.

"Until you're ready to share your work with others, you won't find total fulfillment." Her grandmother's voice echoed in her mind.

Grandmother had perfected her art form, going inward to find the source for her creations and then going outward to share her vision with the world. Julianna couldn't, maybe because her vision was so dark.

She rubbed the back of her neck. Grandmother was probably right. She usually was. But that didn't change anything about the way she felt.

The sound of rapping on the front door intruded on her fruitless thoughts. Wiping her hands on her paint-stained smock, she walked through the archway to the living room and on into the center hall of the elderly Victorian house.

Through the frosted glass of the front door, she saw who it was. Ken.

She probably had paint in her hair. Well, what difference did it make? Annoyed with herself, she stalked to the door and threw it open.

"Ken."

"Hi." He raised his brows. "May I come in? I need to talk with you."

The tension in the back of her neck spread, reaching tentacles toward her forehead. Still, she could hardly tell him to go away.

She stepped back, gesturing to the hallway. "Please."

He came inside, looking around curiously. When he'd picked her up for the powwow she'd been waiting for him on the front porch, not sure she wanted him in her private space.

"Sorry about banging on your door. I rang the bell, but it didn't seem to be working."

She pointed to the dangling wires of the box overhead. "I'm afraid that's something I haven't gotten to yet."

"This place is yours?"

"Every leaking pipe and sagging floor." Now she knew why she hadn't wanted to invite him in. It made her too aware of all the things she should be doing to her house, just to make it livable.

"A handyman's special. Why did you buy it?"

"I didn't. My great-aunt left it to me. Besides, the place has a lot of charm," she added defensively. Poor old house. It didn't deserve to be bad-mouthed. At least it was hers.

"It sure does. Some of these old Victorians have been renovated into real showplaces. Look at that gorgeous old woodwork."

"I've only managed to get the old paint stripped off in the downstairs." She stroked the satiny oak of the newel post. "But it was worth every hour of back-breaking labor."

Ken put his hand next to hers on the post, and her skin warmed as if he'd touched her. "You did a great job." He brushed at her hair. "It looks as if you're painting. I'm sorry to interrupt."

"It's nothing." Suddenly aware of her paint-stained

smock, she stripped it off and tossed it in the corner. "I don't have any dining room furniture, so I use that room as a studio. The light's pretty good in there. Well, it was when I got home from work. It's getting too dark to do any more now. You said you had to talk to me about something?"

"Yes." He shoved his hands into the pockets of the navy Windbreaker he wore. "Jay Nieto."

Tension stiffened her spine. "What about Jay?"

"Look, is there someplace we can sit down? Preferably with some light?"

What was she thinking, keeping him standing in the dim hallway? "Come into the living room." She led the way, thankful that the living room, at least, had been finished.

He paused at the edge of the Navajo rug that covered the polished pine floor, looking around. He let out a low whistle. "Juli, this is beautiful."

She felt her cheeks flush with pleasure at his praise. "It's not typical décor for a Victorian, I'm afraid."

Instead of going with the velvets and needlepoint that would match the architecture, she'd opted for cream walls, a comfortable leather couch with matching chairs, and the pieces of Native American art she'd been collecting since she'd been old enough to understand its beauty.

"No, it's better than that, because it represents you, every inch of it." He crossed to the brown leather chair that was her grandfather's favorite and sat down, looking far too much at home for her comfort.

She sat on the couch opposite him, lacing her fingers together. "What about Jay?"

Ken frowned, his brown eyes darkening. "I ran into him this afternoon. I'm afraid I pushed too hard with him."

She took a breath, biting back the scolding words that hovered on her tongue. Ken might deserve them, but she could feel his regret. Whatever had happened between them, he was obviously sorry for it.

"Tell me."

His level gaze met hers, faint surprise showing. "Aren't you going to start yelling?"

"I'm reserving judgment until I hear the whole thing."

He nodded, the corners of his mouth lifting. "Very fair of you. Well, I was down at the hospital wing site, doing a final check. When I came out, I found Jay outside."

"What was he doing there?" The hospital site was well outside Jay's usual territory, and he didn't drive.

"He said he was looking for me. Trying to find out if you were okay after the accident."

"And you didn't believe him."

"I didn't say that." He paused, as if assessing his reactions. "I think he probably did want to know about you. I figured it was an opportunity to find out if he knew about—" He paused, seeming to run out of words.

"What?" What would put that hesitation in Ken's voice? He always seemed so sure of himself.

"The lightning symbol. I needed to find out if he knew the significance of that to you."

She could only stare at him for a moment. "Why does that matter?"

He leaned toward her, elbows on his knees. "Think about it, Juli. That symbol was put on your computer deliberately. Either we have to believe in the very long arm of coincidence, or the person who put it there knew how much it would rattle you."

In the rush of events, she hadn't even thought that through. She stared numbly at him. "I've really been stupid. I never thought of that." A thought struck her. "You know about the symbol, and what it means to me."

"Your grandmother told me."

In its own way, that was rather astonishing. Her grandmother was one of the most private people she knew, especially when it came to outsiders. Why on earth would she share something like that with Ken? The only answer that occurred to her was one she didn't want to explore.

She rubbed her arms, suddenly chilled. "How did Jay react?"

"As if I'd accused him of something." He shook his head. "Don't bother to yell at me. I should have been more tactful, I guess. But you must see that Jay keeps turning up. As far as I can tell, not many people know the significance of that symbol to you."

"No." It was hardly something she went around talking about. "I suppose, to be honest, Jay might have heard talk about it at the pueblo. But I still can't believe he'd set out to hurt me."

"I hope you're right." He leaned toward her, taking her cold hands in his. "But we have to find out the truth."

"I suppose you're right."

She drew back. The grip of his hands, the nearness

of him, was clouding her thinking. She needed to get a grip—on the effect he had on her and on the pounding in his head.

"Look, I—I have a pot of coffee on. I could stand a cup. How about you?" Maybe the caffeine would help her think straight.

"Sounds good." He leaned back, making no attempt to go with her. Maybe he knew she needed a moment to herself. "Black, please."

She scurried back through the hall to the kitchen. Pulling the bottle of aspirin from the cabinet, she washed two tablets down with water. Then she poured coffee into mugs hand-painted with stylized animal figures, made by one of her grandmother's friends. The familiar actions steadied her.

It was ridiculous to let herself be rattled. If she hadn't been so intent on blocking the memory of that symbol from her mind, she'd have realized the obvious for herself. It wouldn't have had to come from Ken.

Well, they'd think this through together. Ken was right about one thing. If Jay was involved, even innocently, in the things that had been happening, she had to know.

She put the mugs on an enameled tray. Her stomach reminded her that she hadn't eaten since lunch, so she quickly sliced into the fragrant lemon cake her grandmother had sent over. She arranged the slices on a plate and carried the whole thing back to the living room.

Ken wasn't there. For a moment she stood staring at the brown chair where he'd been sitting, and then she realized where he was. The lights were still on in the adjoining studio. He must have gone there.

She set the tray on the side table and crossed quickly to the archway. She didn't choose to share her painting with anyone. Ken didn't have the right to intrude.

She paused in the archway. Ken stood, as she'd known he must, directly in front of her easel, staring at the images she'd captured on canvas. He turned slowly to look at her.

"This is…" he hesitated, as if searching for words, "very powerful. Will you tell me about it?"

"No." She shook her head. "I don't want—" Her throat tightened, her voice thickened.

"Juli—" Ken took a step toward her, face concerned.

Anguish ripped the words from her throat. "I can't! Don't you see? I can't!"

She put shaking hands to her face, appalled that she'd revealed her weakness to him. Hot, bitter tears scalded her. The swirling dark clouds she'd painted seemed to reach out from the canvas as they did in her dreams, as if they'd sweep around her and swallow her whole.

TEN

The anguish in Juli's eyes cut Ken's heart even more than the dark, tumultuous images on the canvas. For a moment he didn't move, struck dumb by the sense that this was pain beyond anything he could help.

But he couldn't just stand by and watch. *Help her,* he murmured silently, able to pray for Juli even if he couldn't pray for himself.

"Juli."

Her palms covered her face, but silent tears dripped through her fingers. Her whole body shook with pain. Still, she made no sound.

Pain twisted his heart. *I don't know what to do for her. Show me.*

Instinct told him she'd be better away from the troubling images she'd put on canvas. He put his arm around her and turned her toward the living room. If she resisted him he wasn't sure what he'd do.

But she moved where he led, docile as a child. He took her to the couch, sitting down beside her. For a moment he hesitated, but this wasn't about what he might feel for Juli as a woman. This was about one human being comforting another. He put his arm around her and drew her close.

She leaned into his shoulder as if hiding, her whole body shaking. He stroked her hair, her back, and sought for words to soothe her.

"I know. I know. It's all right. You're safe."

Nothing very profound, but Juli didn't need profound right now. She just needed to be held, to know someone cared about her. The words his mother used to use when he or Holly had scraped a knee or suffered a broken friendship worked as well as any.

He couldn't see his watch without moving, and he wouldn't disturb her for anything, so he didn't know how long they simply sat, holding each other. Whatever was hurting Juli, he'd guess this storm was a long time building.

Finally the sobs lessened. Her body began to relax against his, her breathing to even out. At last she leaned against the sofa back, limp with exhaustion.

He touched her cheek gently, wiping away the last traces of tears. "I'm sorry you're hurting, but I think maybe you needed that."

She straightened, wiping her cheeks with both palms, gathering the remnants of her dignity around her. "No, I'm sorry. I don't know what happened. I never break down, especially not—"

"In front of someone?"

She nodded.

"Maybe that's a sign you need to talk about it. Maybe I'm not the person you'd choose, but I'm here and I'm ready to listen." He was prodding, very gently. If she slid back behind her protective barriers again, she might never come out.

She clasped her hands in her lap, staring down at them, her face guarded.

He'd have to push harder. He wasn't sure why he knew that was the thing to do, but the impulse was strong. He'd prayed, he realized with surprise. He'd asked for help. Maybe this instinct was the answer.

"Tell me about the painting, Juli."

The way she winced told him that was the trigger.

"Is it something you've actually seen?"

"In nightmares," the words burst out of her. "In my dreams for the past year."

He stroked her back gently. Someone—Michael, it was—had said that she'd had a bad time of it when her unit was deployed to Florida during the hurricanes. He studied the curve of her cheek. She wasn't going to talk unless he forced it.

"I heard you had a tough time a year ago," he said carefully. "Is that where the dreams come from?"

He felt her resistance, felt her straining away from him, struggling to keep the words inside. And he felt the moment when her resistance fell away, when the need to speak became stronger than the urge to hide. She drew in a shaky breath.

"I thought I'd handled it." She shook her head. "I've been to bad scenes before, some worse than that."

"Tell me."

She closed her eyes, but he suspected she saw it anyway, indelibly etched on her mind's eye.

"Angel and I went into a building collapse, looking for survivors." Her shoulders moved slightly, as if shaking something off. "Angel had a scent—I knew it. I followed her in. We found—"

She stopped, her breath rasping.

"What did you find, Juli?" It had been bad, whatever it was.

"A child. A little boy, trapped. I radioed the location. They were coming—I know they were. They dug like madmen. But he was pinned down. There must have been tons of debris over us. No way to get him out."

His hand moved in circles on her back, trying to absorb the pain. "You did your best. No one could do more."

"We couldn't do it." She looked at him then, her eyes dark caverns of grief and regret. "We couldn't get him out. I was holding his hand, talking to him, when I knew he was gone."

The magnitude of it reached out and grabbed his heart, squeezing it in a vise. "It wasn't your fault."

"No. But I failed."

"You didn't fail. You did everything that could be done. You stayed with him and comforted him at the risk of your own life."

She shrugged as if that weren't important. "It wasn't enough." She took a breath, shaking her head a little. "I know. I know all the words. I've said them to other people. I thought I was coping. But then the dreams started. And the fear."

"It's natural to be afraid." He knew that, at least.

"Not like this." Her voice rasped. "When Angel and I go in—" She stopped, as if struggling to find the right words. "When Angel and I used to go in, I'd feel as if we were linked—as if we were one being, as if God guided us to where we needed to be. Now—I just don't feel anything."

"You found my brother and Layla." The thought of losing Michael made his voice rough. "You did what had to be done."

"Angel did it. Not me."

"Angel wouldn't have done it without you."

"I don't know. I just don't have the confidence any longer. I don't know if I can keep on doing it." She swung to face him, her eyes wide and frightened. "What if I never get it back?"

Her words pierced his heart. He knew what that black abyss felt like. What if he could never go back to flying?

Juli was so courageous. He didn't want her to bear this burden alone. But who was he to give anyone else advice when he was trapped by his own weakness?

He had to say something. She was looking at him with such despair.

"You will. You'll get over this. You're already working through the nightmares by painting them out. You're going to be okay, I promise."

A thought struck him, illuminating the darkness like a lightning strike. Did Juli even realize that her painting could also be the image of her mother's death?

If she didn't, he certainly wasn't going to bring it up.

He put his arm around her cautiously, ready to withdraw in an instant if she pulled away. But she turned toward him, relaxing against his shoulder with a small sigh.

"Thank you," she murmured, her voice muffled.

What right did he have to be making promises that this would work out for her? None, probably.

But he could hold her. He could brush a kiss against the smooth skin of her forehead and hold her close. Maybe that was enough for now.

"I still say I don't want you going in a place like that alone." Ken said the words emphatically, and Juli could see that he wasn't going to give up the argument easily.

"We've already been through this." She leaned forward, bracing her hand against the dashboard of the car Ken had borrowed from his mother as she scanned the sidewalks, hoping to spot Jay. "Jay is more likely to respond to me than to you right now. You agreed."

"That was before I saw what this part of town is like."

"It's not the face Colorado Springs wants to show to the tourists, that's for sure."

Ken was frowning. "I remember this as an older, poorer neighborhood, but a decent place for families. What happened to it?"

"Drugs, I'm afraid. Your uncle's cleanup had started to do some good, but since he's been hospitalized it's gone downhill again."

"The sooner Uncle Max gets back to work, the better. That deputy mayor of his seems afraid to do anything." He glanced at her. "Anyway, that's all the more reason why you shouldn't go in that place alone."

"I won't be alone. I'll take Angel." Hearing her name, Angel lifted her head from the backseat and gave a soft woof.

"There's the place." Ken's voice tightened as he nodded to a seedy-looking pool hall in the middle of the next block. "I still say—"

"Please, Ken." She turned toward him as he pulled to the curb. "I'm really worried about Jay. He's so vulnerable right now. I'm afraid almost anything could push him under that gang's control."

"Like my clumsy attempts to play detective, you mean?" He switched off the ignition.

"It's not your fault that Jay's so sensitive. This world is just so different from the one he grew up in. His father loves him and means well. He moved here in the hope he could make enough to send Jay to college. But he's working two jobs, and he just doesn't have the time to spend with the boy." She put her hand on his arm. "I'll be careful."

"You'd better be." He put his hand over hers and gripped it hard. "Because if you're not out of that place in five minutes, I'm coming in."

"Deal." She eyed the dingy glass, behind which dim figures moved. "Believe me, I'm not interested in staying any longer than I have to."

He released her hand reluctantly, it seemed. She slid out of the car and opened the rear door so that Angel could leap out. Quickly, before she could give in to second thoughts, she walked toward the pool hall door, which seemed to stand perpetually ajar.

She paused for a moment once she'd stepped inside,

letting her eyes adjust to the dim light. The room smelled of stale cigarette smoke and a few other aromas she declined to identify.

The place wasn't that crowded this early in the evening. Action and sound, which had stopped abruptly when she came in, resumed.

Jay leaned against the wall at the rear of the room, apparently watching two older teens shooting pool. She walked straight to him, ignoring comments that flowed in her wake. Angel stuck to her heels.

"Jay."

He straightened, dark eyes wary. "Juli. What are you doing here?"

"Looking for you. We have to talk."

He fidgeted, not meeting her eyes. "Now's not a good time."

"Seems like a very good time to me." She touched his arm, finding it so tense it seemed to shoot sparks. "Come on."

"Hey, Nieto. Who's your girlfriend?"

The jeering voice came from one of the players. He turned away from the table to face them, and Juli's mouth went dry. She didn't need an introduction to know this must be Theo Crale.

Jay seemed frozen in place, like a rabbit hypnotized by a snake.

Snake. The word sent an inner shudder through her. That was what Crale reminded her of. A dangerous snake.

She wouldn't let him think he intimidated her. "I'm Julianna Red Feather. Who are you?"

"Ju-li-anna." He mocked her, spinning her name out

with a sensual air. "Well, hey, pretty Julianna, come here and I'll show you how to play."

Snickers came from the others. Jay blinked. "Leave her alone. Go on, Juli. Get out of here."

"*You* get out, Nieto. Your pretty friend stays." He reached toward her.

She tensed, hand tight on Angel's ruff, feeling the low growl start in the dog's throat.

She held her breath. She wasn't afraid for herself, not with Angel at her side and Ken just outside. But Jay—

Jay knocked Crale's hand away. "I said, leave her alone!"

Like a snake striking, Crale grabbed Jay's shirt, fist pulling back. "You sure you want to interfere, stupid?"

Jay glared back at him. "You're the stupid one if you plan to take on Juli Red Feather. That dog will tear you to pieces."

Angel had never attacked anyone in her life, but Crale didn't know that. Juli loosened her grip on the collar slightly. Angel lunged forward, baring her teeth.

Crale stumbled back a step, bumping into the table. Encouraged, Angel barked at him.

"Quiet, Angel." She looked at Jay, pride welling in her at the boy's response. "Shall we get out of here?"

"That's right, get out," Crale snarled. "Don't come around anymore, Nieto. You're not wanted." He added a few words Juli decided she'd rather not hear.

"Fine by me," Jay said. Holding Juli's arm, he steered her through the silent bystanders toward the door.

When they reached it, they found Ken waiting. Juli lifted her eyebrows. "It hasn't been five minutes, has it?"

"It seemed like a year, but I guess I didn't need to worry about you, not with Angel and Jay to protect you." He put his hand on Jay's shoulder. "Come on. Let's get out of here. I'll buy you both supper."

If Jay hesitated, it was only for an instant. His shy smile lit his face. "Can we get pizza?"

Thanksgiving flooded her soul. *Thank You, Lord.*

Jay had hit a crossroads in his life, and he'd turned in the right direction.

"I'm glad we got here in time to see the noon formation."

Ken said the words that were appropriate to the occasion, but Juli wasn't sure he meant them. His eyes were hidden behind his dark sunglasses, but the tautness to his jaw said that the Air Force Academy was the last place on earth he wanted to be right now.

"It's certainly impressive," Juli murmured, watching the uniformed cadets marching in unison along the paved rectangles of the Academy grounds. Her heart seemed to swell as the flag went by.

Still, she didn't particularly want to be here either. Hadn't she decided that further contact with Ken would lead straight to heartache? But when he'd offered to bring Jay on a tour, he and Jay had clearly thought that included her. She hadn't had the heart to say no.

Be honest with yourself, her inner voice declared. *No matter what the eventual cost, you plan to enjoy this day to the fullest.*

The last group went by. Jay watched until they were

out of sight, and then turned to Ken, his eyes shining. "That was awesome."

"Well, you might lose a little of the thrill when you've done it a few hundred times. This way—let's walk over to the chapel. Juli will like to see that. Unless you've done the tour before?" He looked at her, making it a question.

"No, I never have." She'd felt a little strange when Ken had driven through the North Gate, as if someone would stop and ask them what right they had to be here.

He gave her a look of mock horror. "You've lived in Colorado Springs most of your life and you've never seen the local sights?"

"You know how it is. Tourists come from around the world to see this, and locals never even think to take the tour." She shrugged. "I guess it is funny. I mean, The Springs is such a military town."

"Yes. It's impossible to get away from the signs of that."

His voice had that tense note again, and she didn't know what to say. Ken's whole being was tied up in his career. If he couldn't have that, how could he stand to face the daily reminders?

Jay had hurried on ahead of them, impatient with their slow pace.

"Do you think he was telling us the truth?" Ken's gaze was on Jay, his voice low.

"I think so. I hope so." She frowned, trying to get her mind around that difficult conversation they'd had with Jay once they'd gotten safely away from the pool hall. "I believe he didn't participate in any vandalism, that's for sure. But did he let anything drop that might have given Crale ideas…well, that's harder to say."

"He did know about the connotation that particular symbol had for you."

She nodded, disliking the thought that people had been talking about her. "I guess it's natural enough that people at the pueblo still talked about my mother's death. The Zuni are great storytellers."

"It's hard to be the subject of that sort of story, though."

Ken did understand her feelings.

"The thing I don't get is why." They'd been over it and over it, and she still didn't understand. "Even if we assume Crale had something to do with the vandalism, what was the point? And why fiddle with the computer that way? He can't have had any idea of what the effect of tampering with the financial reports would be."

"It doesn't seem likely. But we can't ignore the fact that someone could have paid him to do it."

"But who? And why?"

He shrugged. "A vendetta against Montgomery Construction? I know it seems unlikely, but so do all the other nasty things that have been happening."

"No one could hope to harm the construction company by tampering with the brakes on your car." She still got a chill at how close they'd come that night.

"A vendetta against Montgomerys and Vances then." His mouth twisted. "If I heard anyone else say that, I'd think he was suffering from paranoia."

"You know how the saying goes. 'It's not paranoia if someone really is out to get you.'"

"Well, the situation is in the capable hands of my

police detective cousin now. We'll have to trust him to put it all together."

"I hope he can." Still, what did Sam Vance have to go on? A lot of random, ugly incidents that didn't seem to lead anywhere.

Ken paused, pointing ahead. "That's the chapel. You've probably seen it on postcards, at least."

"I'm happy to say I have, but the postcards don't give you any idea of the scale."

The building shone silver in the sunlight, shaped like a row of fighter jets, their noses pointed toward the sky. Her heart winced. Was that yet another reminder for Ken?

While she stood staring at it, Jay had stopped at a fighter plane, mounted in the grass at the edge of the walkway. Ken went to join him, and she could hear him answering the boy's eager questions. Jay wouldn't catch the strain in Ken's voice, but she did.

She went toward them. "I thought we were going to see the chapel."

Ken nodded, turning his back on the plane too quickly. Maybe that was why he had wanted her here today—to serve as a buffer against the pain of Jay's enthusiasm.

"Look!" Jay's voice brimmed with excitement as he pointed up.

Her breath caught. A group of gliders soared over them silently, crystal clear against the blue sky. With their slender wings and long noses, they looked like a flight of prehistoric birds.

"It's the aerobatic team," Ken said. "Practicing maneuvers."

"Were you in that?" Jay's voice was filled with awe.

"I was."

She heard the pain in his voice, and her heart hurt for him.

"I'm sorry," she said softly, as Jay wandered away, head tilted back to watch the gliders.

"For what?" His tone was brittle.

"It's hard for you to be here. But it was such a good thing to do for Jay." She looked into her heart and found a sliver of what might be jealousy. "You've done so much more for that boy than I ever could."

He shrugged. "Just because he's flying-mad. You and Angel would outscore me with any kid who wasn't."

"I don't think that's all it is." She couldn't explain to him what she felt, and wouldn't if she could. But she and Jay both understood.

There was a difference between being born Julianna Red Feather, with a disappearing father who hadn't even bothered to give her his name, and being born Kenneth Vance, with all that name meant in Colorado Springs.

Ken didn't see, and that fact was a credit to him. But she did. She'd best hold on to that difference, and not let herself get caught up in memories of Ken holding her. Of Ken kissing her. Because that wasn't going to lead anywhere at all.

ELEVEN

"I think it needs to boil just a tad longer." Holly bent over the glass of water on the counter, staring intently at the tiny glob of chocolate she'd just dropped in.

"You're the fudge expert, not I." Juli glanced at her friend. Holly had shown up unexpectedly at her door a few evenings after that trip to the Air Force Academy, declaring that her husband was working late, that she was totally bored with the restrictions on her activities and that she needed distraction.

Holly grinned. "I haven't made fudge since I was about thirteen. Mom and I went through a run of making candy together. That was probably the only way she could get me to have a conversation with her at that age."

"My grandmother was the cook at our house, but I don't remember ever making fudge with her. Corn bread, lots of corn bread." She finished buttering the platter she'd gotten out at Holly's direction.

"There, perfect." Holly lifted the saucepan from the burner and began spreading the thick, glossy chocolate on the platter. The aroma was so rich that even Angel, lying on her favorite spot on a braided rug in front of the sink, raised her head and sniffed.

"None for you," Juli said. "Chocolate isn't good for dogs."

"That means we'll have to eat it ourselves." Holly swirled a design into the surface with a knife. "Seriously, didn't you make fudge at all those pajama parties we had when we were in school?"

"No." That came out too harshly. "I mean, I wasn't invited to any pajama parties." She remembered only too well hearing the popular girls, the girls like Holly, chatter about the parties to which she'd never been invited.

Holly paused, knife poised over the fudge. "I'm sorry. That was stupid of me. I wish I'd made an effort to get to know you when we were both in school."

"Stop, or I'll start feeling sorry for myself." She looked back at the person she'd once been. "Probably every teenage girl in the world sometimes feels she doesn't belong. I was just so sure I wasn't acceptable that I hid instead of trying to find a friend."

Holly plopped a square of warm fudge onto a napkin and handed it to her. "There, try that and tell me it's wonderful."

She took a cautious bite. The aroma and taste seemed to explode in her mouth as the chocolate melted on her tongue. "Wonderful doesn't do it justice."

Angel sat up, whining a little, and she shook her head at the dog. "Chocolate is only for humans, Angel."

Holly slid onto a chair, taking a huge mouthful of fudge. "Ah, that's what I was craving," she said thickly.

"Seriously, though, Juli, I'm glad we're friends now." She wiggled the silver bracelet on her wrist. "Only a friend would have made my brother get me this gorgeous bracelet."

"I didn't make him. It was entirely his idea."

Holly's eyebrows lifted. "He wouldn't have thought of it if the bracelets hadn't been put under his nose. Believe me, I know my twin. So, what do you think of Ken now that you've gotten to know him as an adult?" The question was so carelessly put that Juli wondered if that was the real reason Holly had come.

"I'm happy to have him for a friend," she said firmly. He wouldn't have told Holly about the moments when she'd cried in his arms, would he? No, of course he wouldn't.

Angel, as if sensing her troubled thoughts, clicked across the floor to her, putting her muzzle on Juli's knee. She rubbed Angel's ears gently.

"Well, since we're all friends now, why haven't you responded yet to the invitation to Michael and Layla's engagement party?"

She could hardly say she'd looked at the invitation everyday, wondering why she'd been invited and what she should do about it. Or that the thought of a horde of Vances and Montgomerys en masse gave her hives.

"Sorry. I guess I should have called you by now with an answer."

"You should." Holly smiled. "And since I'm here, you can tell me that you're coming. Mom and I have to go out to Cripple Creek early to set things up, but Ken will be happy to drive you."

She didn't think she responded in any visible way to that suggestion, but Angel pulled away, looked at her reproachfully and padded to the door.

"I have to let Angel out," she said quickly, and went to open the back door.

She stood for a moment, holding the door open, letting the cool evening air into the warm kitchen. If Holly was still trying to play matchmaker for her and Ken—

A volley of furious barking from the backyard interrupted her thoughts. Holly's chair scraped as she stood.

"What is it? What's Angel barking at?"

"I don't know. Could be another dog." But a frisson of fear went down her spine. That didn't sound like Angel's greeting to another animal.

She threw the switch to the back porch light. Nothing happened. The backyard remained shrouded in darkness.

She grabbed the flashlight from its hook by the door. "Stay here." She pulled the door open and ran out, fumbling with the switch of the flashlight.

She smacked her shin on something on the back porch. There should have been nothing there—she didn't leave things on the narrow porch. Skipping the two steps, she jumped to the ground, finally finding the flashlight switch.

The strong beam of the light cut through the darkness. She swung it around the small yard. Nothing. Where was Angel?

Another furious volley of barking answered her. It came from the side of the house that bordered the alley.

Just as she turned, Angel's barking cut off with a yelp of pain.

Heart pounding, she raced toward the side yard. *Please, Lord, please, Lord.*

She rounded the house full tilt, the beam of the flashlight bouncing crazily. From the corner of her eye she caught the movement of a dark-clad figure disappearing over the fence.

Then her light hit Angel, and the breath went out of her. Angel lay on her side, motionless, and blood formed a pool around her head.

Ken charged in the door of the veterinary hospital, stomach twisted in the knots that had taken up permanent residence since Holly called him. He wasn't sure who he was worried about most—Holly, or Juli, or Angel.

Then he got into the waiting room and he knew. Juli. Juli was the one who needed him now. Holly had gone home wrapped in her husband's strong arms, and Angel was in the capable hands of the vet. But Juli—Juli was alone.

She sat in one of the straight wooden chairs that were arranged along the wall, hands clasped in her lap, lips moving silently. Praying for Angel.

He crossed to her in a few quick strides and sat next to her, folding his hands over hers. Hers were so cold it startled him.

"Juli."

She looked up at him, her eyes piteously pleading, like a hurt child's. "I was praying."

"I know. I've been praying since I heard." He

wrapped his hands more securely around hers, trying to warm her. "Everyone has. Have you heard anything about her condition?"

Her throat moved with the effort of swallowing. "Not yet. She's in surgery. That's all I know."

"I'm so sorry."

She nodded, taking a deep breath as if to steady herself. "Holly. Is she okay?"

"She's fine. I got hold of Jake and he took her home. She wouldn't go until I promised I'd stay with you. Not that I wouldn't have, in any event."

"What—" She paused, moistened her lips, and seemed to make an effort to speak naturally. "Did the police catch him?"

"No. They found—" Now he was the one who had to force himself to speak naturally over the rage that clogged his throat. "They found a pile of oily rags and trash on your back porch, and a can of kerosene nearby. His intent was pretty clear. If Angel hadn't heard him, he'd have torched the house."

He didn't want to think about how quickly that old wooden structure would have gone up. Fury burned along his nerves. Holly and Juli had been in the kitchen. Would they have gotten out?

"She saved our lives." Juli seemed to have no doubts. "Maybe at the cost of her own." Her voice broke, and tears dripped down onto their clasped hands.

He'd never seen strong, capable Juli so vulnerable. He longed to take her in his arms, but if he did— If he did, he'd be saying they had a relationship closer than friendship, and he didn't think either of them was ready for that.

"You got her here quickly. Layla says Doc Stewart is the best veterinary surgeon in town, and she should know."

His brother's veterinarian fiancé had wanted to make the drive from Cripple Creek the instant she heard, but she'd realized that immediate care was crucial.

Juli nodded, her hands clasping his. They seemed a little warmer, and he was grateful for that small sign. "He volunteers with the search-and-rescue team. He's the best, but Angel looked so bad."

"She's in good hands," he said firmly. "Don't think about anything else." He tried to think of something, anything, that would distract her, keep her from sinking into despair. "Quinn wanted me to tell you he'll clean everything up at the house as soon as the police let him. And he's posting a guard there at night."

"He doesn't have to do that. It's not his responsibility."

"It's our responsibility. You wouldn't have been targeted if not for your relationship with us."

"You don't know that. It could have been—" She stopped, frowning.

"What? Who?"

"I was thinking of that clash with Theo Crale. It seems far-fetched, but—"

"It's not far-fetched at all. I told Sam about it, and he's going to question the creep. But after the fires last month, it seems more likely to be connected to the Vances and Montgomerys, doesn't it?"

"I suppose." She didn't sound completely convinced, but at least she was thinking about something other than Angel's chance of survival.

The door to the exam rooms swung open, and Juli

shot to her feet. He got up, too, putting his arm around her waist. If the news was bad he didn't know how he'd comfort her.

But Dr. Stewart managed a tired smile. "I think she's going to be okay, Juli. The surgery was touch and go, but she hung in there. She's a fighter."

Juli sagged against him. "Are you sure?"

"Sure as I can be. We'll watch her closely, but I expect a full recovery." He ran a hand through thinning hair. "If I could get my hands on the person who did this—"

"You'll have to get in line, Doc." He tightened his grip on Juli, not liking the ashy hue of her face. "Juli, she's going to be all right. Hang on to that."

She nodded. "Can I see her?"

"Just for a second." The vet stepped back, holding the door wide. "You can both take a brief look, and then your friend had better take you home. Don't worry, I'm not going anywhere."

Arm still around Juli, Ken walked with her into the operating room. A technician, who was cleaning up, smiled at them and then tactfully withdrew.

Angel lay motionless, swathed in bandages. Juli reached out a careful hand and stroked her foreleg.

"It's okay, sweetheart." Her voice choked. "You're going to be all right."

"Come on." Ken tightened his grasp, half-afraid she was going to keel over. "I'm sure they have things to do."

He led her out to the waiting room, his heart twisting with her vulnerability. She seemed so alone. The perpetrator had taken away her main source of protection, for the time being, at least.

One thing was sure—she couldn't go back to that house alone.

"Look, Juli, how about coming home with me? Mom would be delighted to put you up."

She shook her head. "I'll be all right."

"You shouldn't be alone."

"She won't be."

He hadn't heard the door open, but he looked up to see Juli's grandfather filling the opening. With a little cry, Juli launched herself at him, and he enfolded her in his arms.

"It's all right, little one." He stroked her back, his face filled with love and tenderness. "It's all right." He glanced at Ken. "Thanks for the offer, but Juli will come home to us."

Ken nodded, trying to ignore an irrational sense of disappointment. Juli's grandparents were her family. Naturally she'd want to be with them now.

But he couldn't help wishing he was the one she turned to for comfort.

Juli drove down the narrow dirt lane to the Double V ranch outside Cripple Creek, wishing she'd been able to find some reasonable excuse why she couldn't come to Michael and Layla's engagement party. She hadn't been able to, not without running the risk of hurting Holly, so here she was, headed toward a social engagement that made her palms wet.

It almost seemed that Holly had been more shaken by the arson attempt and Angel's injury than Juli had. She'd called three times a day since then, checking on Juli, and had been openly relieved that both Juli and Angel were staying with Julie's grandparents for a few days.

At least she'd been able to evade Holly's repeated suggestions that Ken drive her to the party. She'd insisted on driving herself, saying that she didn't want to leave Angel for long and she wouldn't make anyone else leave early for her sake.

That wasn't the real reason, and she knew it. The truth was that she'd made herself far too vulnerable to Ken, just as she had back in high school. The fact that they knew and understood each other better now didn't really make a difference.

They were still separated by every conceivable barrier—class, race, upbringing, personal history, dreams for the future. She couldn't betray her love for Ken when she was still struggling through an emotional crisis, any more than it would be fair for him to begin a relationship when he was fighting his own battle for his future.

The barns loomed on her left, and then she saw the ranch house, its lights glowing their warm welcome. What seemed like dozens of cars lined the sides of the lane, and Juli felt her breathing grow a bit shallower.

Montgomerys and Vances, who knew how many of them, crowded the small house. If she'd thought she'd gotten over the insecurity of her high school years, she'd been wrong.

Okay, she could do this. She pulled to a parking space at the end of the row. That would allow her to make a quick getaway. She'd go in, chat for a few minutes, make her excuses and leave.

She picked up the gift she'd brought—a handmade pottery piece created by a friend of her grandmother's—slid out of the car and started for the front porch, heart thumping louder with each step.

The front door stood open, with the sound of country music almost drowned out by the flood of voices. Gripping the package a little tighter, she stepped inside and felt instantly swallowed up by the crowd.

She spotted Quinn, and a moment later he arrived at her side, giving her a quick hug.

"Holly said you were coming, but I said I wouldn't believe it until I saw you myself. How are you doing?"

"I'm fine, really." She probably should have gone back to work before this, but she hadn't been able to bring herself to leave Angel. "I'll be back at work on Monday, I promise."

He gave her a searching look. "Not unless it's really what you want. I can't help but feel responsible, and your well-being, and Angel's, is more important than keeping the records straight."

Tears stung her eyes, and she blinked them away. Her emotions had been way too close to the surface lately. "Nobody needs to feel responsible except for the guilty person. Are there any leads yet?"

He shrugged. "If so, Sam hasn't been willing to share them. And I've been too busy at the site to hound him about it. We're really coming down to the wire."

Now she was the one to feel guilty. Quinn had been good to her. The fate of his company was hanging in the balance, and she'd been staying home and letting her grandmother pamper her instead of doing what she could.

"How is it going? Will you make the deadline?"

"If nothing else happens." He grinned. "There might still be some wet paint and unfinished offices when they hold the ribbon-cutting, but I don't suppose anyone will sue us over that."

"I will be back at work on Monday," she said firmly. "And if there's anything extra you need, just ask."

"Thanks, Julianna." He glanced at the package she clutched. "There's a table against the wall for gifts, if you want to put that down. I'd show you, but I'm supposed to be getting a plate from the buffet for my mother."

"Go." She shooed him away. "I'm fine."

But once he'd disappeared, she felt adrift in a sea of people she didn't really know. People smiled and nodded, but for the most part they didn't know her any better than she knew them.

She reached the gift table and slid her package to an inconspicuous spot. Maybe she could just slip away. After all, she'd made an appearance, hadn't she? She turned away from the table and nearly walked right into Ken.

Her breath caught, and she could only hope he didn't realize that. He smiled, his face warming with what seemed to be pleasure at the sight of her.

"Juli. You came."

Why did everyone seem surprised? "I said I would."

His fingers closed over her wrist, sending a flood of warmth running straight to her heart. "You wouldn't let me bring you. I thought maybe you were going to back out on us at the last minute."

It was hard to keep her voice even when her heart

was beating a wild drum rhythm. "I just can't stay long, that's all. Angel gets restless when I'm not there."

"You can't leave until you've talked to Michael and Layla." He pulled her arm firmly through his, tucking it closely against his side. "Come on. I'll take you over."

She had no choice but to keep step with him. In fact, she probably couldn't have pulled away if she'd wanted to. *Enjoy the moment,* she told herself. *It will end soon.*

Michael and Layla stood in front of the huge stone fireplace, fielding congratulations and kidding from their friends and relatives.

"That's Colleen Montgomery, Quinn's cousin, talking to them," Ken murmured in her ear.

"I know. I met her when she did a story on the search-and-rescue team for the newspaper. She's a good reporter, from what I hear."

Ken grinned. "She rushes in where angels fear to tread, as the saying goes. Sam's taken to avoiding her every chance he gets, for fear she'll start bugging him about the investigation."

"Who's the man next to her?" A tall, dark-haired man had put his hand lightly on Colleen's shoulder.

"Alessandro Donato." Ken's voice was carefully non-committal, as if he didn't want to show a bias for or against the man. "He's my aunt Lidia's nephew, but I don't know him very well." He shook his head, dismissing his cousin-by-marriage. "Mike and Layla look happy, don't they?"

"Definitely."

Michael's normally taciturn face was suffused with love when he looked at his fiancée, and as for Layla—

well, if anyone had been more in love, Juli hadn't seen it. The glow that surrounded them seemed strong enough to heat the whole house.

Colleen and Alessandro moved away, and Michael and Layla spotted them.

"Julianna!" Layla enveloped her in a flutter of turquoise silk, her hug warm. "We're so happy you're here."

Michael took her hand in his as soon as Layla released her. "After all, we wouldn't be here to have this party if it weren't for you and Angel. How's she doing?"

She felt warmth in her cheeks at his praise. "She's doing much better, thanks."

Layla clutched her arm. "I have a homeopathic remedy that will do wonders for her. I'll get it to you."

"Thanks so much. That's kind of you." She wasn't quite sure what Dr. Stewart would think of that, but surely it couldn't hurt. And people did say that Layla's unconventional methods worked wonders.

Someone else came up to greet the happy couple just then, and Juli was happy to step back into the crowd. Ken bent his head to hers.

"That's Layla's parents over by the buffet. You should introduce yourself."

She probably could have picked the couple out without any help. With their flowing clothes and long, graying hair, they looked transported from the sixties.

"I really can't stay long," she repeated.

Ken squeezed her arm. "I have a few best man chores to take care of. Get something to eat, and I'll catch up with you before you go."

He slipped away, and she followed the progress of

his tall figure through the crowd. Best man—she hadn't thought of that, but of course he'd be his brother's best man.

She spotted Holly and began to work her way through the crowd to her. She'd say hello to Holly, so her friend would know she'd kept her word. And then she'd slip out the nearest door.

As she approached, Jake seemed to notice her. He put his arm around Holly protectively, turning her slightly away, as if to protect Holly from her.

She stopped, stunned for a moment. Well, that reaction was natural enough, if she thought about it rationally. Jake probably didn't even realize he'd done it. He was simply acting out of his instinctive need to protect his wife and baby.

Holly hadn't noticed her, and a couple Juli didn't know came up to claim Holly's attention. Juli stood still, letting the crowd swirl around her. Holly was where she belonged, surrounded by people who loved her. Maybe it was time she did that, too—went home to people who loved her. She'd make her apologies to Ken at work.

She went quickly to the door and hurried out. She paused on the porch, taking a deep breath of cool air and letting her eyes adjust to the dark. Footsteps sounded behind her, and before she could move, Ken was beside her.

"Hey, no fair. You weren't leaving without saying goodbye, were you?"

"I really need to get home." That didn't sound convincing, even to her.

A burst of laughter came from the open doorway, and

Ken glanced back toward the party with a frown. "I'll walk you out to your car."

She was too aware of his tall figure next to her as they moved out of the circle of yellow light from the porch. Stubbly grass brushed against her ankles. Away from the city lights, the sky was incredibly black, the stars even more incredibly bright.

Ken slowed, tilting his head back. "Almost looks as if you could touch them, doesn't it?"

"Yes." She felt the tension ease out of her in the stillness. "I'm sorry about running out. I really was concerned about Angel, but frankly, I'm not too good with crowds."

"They are rather overwhelming, aren't they?" He nodded, as if in sympathy. "The whole bunch has known each other for years. They forget that everyone else doesn't know them as well. So tell me, how does Angel like staying at your grandparents?"

"She's being thoroughly spoiled, I'm afraid."

"She deserves it. She may have saved your life." He turned to face her. "If anything had happened to you—"

He stopped, as if they were words he didn't want to say.

"It didn't." She tried to say it lightly. "We're all fine."

"But you could have been hurt, maybe killed." His voice had softened to a baritone rumble that seemed to reach into her soul. "Juli, I—"

He shook his head, lifted his hand, and caressed her cheek.

The world stopped. She was still breathing, wasn't

she? Maybe not—at least, not when he lowered his head and found her lips.

It was like lightning, the current that swept between them. But this lightning didn't frighten her. Instead, it warmed her thoroughly. She felt his arms go around her, protecting, cherishing.

She loved him. She had to tell him, had to say—

He pulled away suddenly, and her lips were cold where his had been.

"I'm sorry." He took a step back. "I shouldn't have done that."

She fought for control. Fought to smile, to say something that would treat it lightly.

She couldn't. She could only stare at his face, shadowed in the moonlight.

He'd broken her heart once before. She should be used to it. She should be immune. But she wasn't.

She finally managed a smile. "Good night, Ken." She turned and fled to the car.

TWELVE

Ken leaned forward in his chair, rubbing the back of his neck where tension had gathered. He'd been closeted with Quinn and Sam in Quinn's office for nearly an hour, and it seemed they were getting nowhere.

For the past few days he'd been occupied full time in trying to help with Sam's investigation. At least, he called it helping. He wasn't sure Sam saw it that way.

"The bottom line is that I'm sure in my own mind that Theo Crale is the man we're looking for in the attack at Julianna's house," Sam said, leaning forward in his chair, his face drawn with frustration. "Unfortunately the lab boys haven't been able to come up with any hard evidence linking him to the crime."

Quinn was frowning. "Where does he claim he was at the time?"

"He says he was with his boys. Naturally they back him up, for all that's worth."

"So we do nothing, and he's free to try again?" Quinn's frustration showed in his voice.

"I tried to put a scare into him." Sam shrugged. "But he's such a hard case he doesn't scare easily. Look, I'm not giving up on this, but I have to be honest with you on where it stands."

Quinn moved restlessly in his chair. "I've lived through the results of arson. I don't like the feeling we're doing nothing."

"Believe me, I'd love to tie the arson attempt at Juli's with the fire here, but I can't. If we could—"

"Never mind what you can't do." The tension was building into a pounding in Ken's head, and his voice was so harsh the other two looked at him in surprise. "How are we going to protect Juli?"

"I've got someone watching the house at night," Quinn reminded him. "And as long as she's staying with her grandparents, I think she's safe."

An image of Juli's grandfather flickered through his mind. Maybe Harvey wasn't as young as he used to be, but Ken suspected he could hold his own against any young punk.

"Maybe so, but she won't stay there long. She's too independent for that. As soon as she feels Angel is okay, she'll be back in her own house. Then what?"

He glanced toward the door to the outer office, wondering if she'd come in yet. They'd hoped to get through this early morning meeting before Juli arrived, to wonder and worry about the nebulous results of the investigation.

"We can't stop her from going home." Sam rose, grabbing his jacket from the back of his chair. "When she goes back, I'll make sure there are increased patrols down her street. That's about all I can do, other than trying to catch the perp." He gripped Ken's shoulder briefly. "I'm trying, Ken."

"I know." He hated to put Sam on the spot, but fear for Juli's safety rode him relentlessly. "Thanks, Sam."

Sam nodded. "Take care. I'll be in touch." He went out.

Quinn studied him for a moment. "You're worried about Julianna."

"Of course I am. Aren't you?"

"Sure. But I don't think I'm taking it quite so personally."

Personally? Quinn had a point. But then, Quinn didn't know about that kiss. And he wouldn't.

Ken stood, restless, needing to move.

"We're friends. I care what happens to her." He'd like to believe Quinn would accept that and let the subject drop, but suspected he wouldn't.

Quinn nodded slowly. "I can see that. I just—well, I don't want Julianna to get hurt. In any way."

Ken stiffened. "There's nothing between us, if that's what you mean."

"Why not?" Quinn shrugged. "I mean, a blind man could see that you're attracted to each other. So, why not?"

"Attraction doesn't mean you're right for each other. Now…well, now the timing isn't right for me to get involved with anyone." He frowned. "What is this, advice to the lovelorn? I don't mess with your love life."

Quinn grinned. "Only because I don't have one." He raised his hands. "All right, I'll butt out. You're a big boy now. You ought to know what you're doing."

He ought to. He turned away from Quinn, heading for the door. He surely ought to.

He'd been crazy to kiss Juli, crazy to let himself be drawn to her. He couldn't deny the attraction he felt for her. Or the admiration.

But he was floundering—at odds with God for the blow life had dealt him. He wouldn't risk hurting Juli by acting out of his own needs instead of what was right for both of them.

He swung the door open to the outer office. If he'd timed it right, he'd be off to the hospital site before Juli arrived, and that was probably best for both of them, even if it did leave him feeling like there was a huge emptiness where she should be.

He crossed the office quickly, grabbed the handle to the outer door and opened it just as Juli reached for it. She took a step, her eyes darkening at the sight of him.

"Hi." It cost him to keep his voice even and his smile neutral when all he really wanted to do was put his arms around her. "How's everything? Is Angel doing okay?"

He stepped aside, letting her come in while he held the door open, ready for his escape.

"Fine." She didn't look at him as she crossed to her desk and put her bag down. She wore that impassive expression she did so well, but he'd seen the flash of emotion, of vulnerability, in her eyes. "She's eager to be back in action. We've started taking her outside for some gentle exercise."

"You're still at your grandparents' house, aren't you?"

She nodded. "We'll probably go home soon, though. I don't like leaving my place empty."

"Juli—" He didn't have the right to say it, but he was

going to, anyway. "Don't be in a rush, okay? You're safer with your grandparents until the police get a handle on this situation."

"I'm not going to hide because of a stupid coward like Crale."

"A stupid, dangerous coward," he said.

"I'll be fine. Don't worry about me." There was finality to the words. What she was really saying was you don't have the right to give me advice.

And she was right. He didn't.

"I'll be down at the hospital site if you need me for anything."

He stepped outside, closing the door. If Juli needed anything, he was the last person she'd call. That was for the best, but it sure didn't feel good.

That had certainly been a wasted trip. Juli crossed from the cabinetry department back to the office, fuming a little. She'd been ready to leave for the day when Dahlia Sainsbury had called from the museum. She'd been convinced that something was wrong about the design and had insisted that Julianna go and check it out. A phone call wouldn't do—she'd only trust a visual inspection.

Since Quinn was busy elsewhere, Juli had gone, and there hadn't been a thing wrong with the design. She suspected that her voice had been a bit tart when she'd called the woman back to tell her that.

Well, forget Dahlia. That was easy. Forget Ken—that was considerably more difficult.

He'd made his feelings crystal clear when he'd

apologized for kissing her. Anything between them was a mistake. Fine. That was just what she'd been telling herself.

Now, if she could just convince her foolish heart of that. Oh, she'd get over her feelings for him eventually. But she couldn't help grieving for what might have been.

She hurried back into her office. She would shut down the computer, lock up and head home. With a bit of luck when it came to the traffic, she'd be back at her grandparents' in time to take Angel out for some exercise before dark. That would do them both some good.

A scribbled note lay in the center of her desk. It read: Ken Vance called. Meet him at the hospital site as soon as possible.

She frowned, stared at it and then picked up the receiver and dialed Ken's cell phone. If she had to fight traffic clear down to Vance Memorial, she'd never get home before dark. Maybe Ken's problem was something she could deal with from here.

But the call went straight to his voice mail. She left a brief message, knowing that was no help. Frowning, she crossed the hall to check with the two women who worked in sales. If she could find out who'd taken the message, maybe she'd know what it was about.

But the office was empty—even Quinn was gone. It looked as if she'd be running down to the hospital site, like it or not.

Traffic was just as bad as she'd expected, and by the time she reached the site, dusk already drew in, casting shadows on the stark structure. She hadn't been to the site in over a week, and she was amazed at how much had been completed.

She parked at the curb and picked her way across a muddy patch to a wooden walkway into the building. No sidewalks yet, but probably those were among the last things to be finished.

The place looked deserted. Obviously the workers had gotten away from their job faster than she had hers. She stepped inside and found herself in the rotunda, where a wide center staircase led to the upper floors. She remembered enough of the plans to know that the reception area and lobby would be here, looking as welcoming as any hotel lobby.

"Hello?" She called out, expecting to hear Ken's answering hail. All she heard was the echo of her own voice, floating down from above like the dust motes that drifted in the last rays of sunlight.

She walked across the rotunda floor, her flat heels clicking on the marble floor. It was still covered with dust, but its beauty showed through. She stopped at the bottom of the steps, looking up the stairwell.

She'd seen sketches of the design, of course, but they hadn't done justice to the grace and strength of the design. This would be a triumph for Montgomery Construction, if they could just get it finished in time.

"Ken!" she called, louder now. There was nobody to disturb, and she needed to find Ken and finish up before it was too dark to see anything in the building. "Ken, where are you? It's Juli."

A sound echoed down the stairwell from high above. Ken, presumably, calling her name. She started up the stairs. Apparently the problem he'd discovered, whatever it was, was on the top floor.

The issue that brought her here must be important. Ken had made it obvious that he was no more eager to see her than she was to see him. Kissing her had been a mistake, and it embarrassed him to be around her now.

The way he'd been embarrassed to be around her in high school? He'd tried to be kind to her then, but she'd known the truth about how he felt. And now history was repeating itself, as if the wheel of time, turning, had brought both of them back to where they'd started.

She reached the top floor finally and took a few cautious steps away from the stairwell. This area was unfinished, littered with stacks of lumber, strewn with the debris of all the projects under way, turned into a maze by hanging sheets of plastic that swayed in the currents of air from the holes where windows would go.

Naturally she didn't have a flashlight—she hadn't thought to bring one from the car. Walking through this mess would be like picking her way through a debris field, and she didn't have on the shoes for it.

"Ken, where are you? It's getting dark."

"Back here."

The shouted words gave her a direction at least. She started toward the sound, stumbling on a board left in a pile of sawdust. "Do you have a light?"

No answer. She frowned. Had he moved out of earshot? Surely he'd realize that it was difficult to find him in this jungle. She pushed aside a hanging sheet of plastic, only to be confronted by several more.

This was like being in a fun house. And she didn't like fun houses.

"Ken?" she called again.

Like an answer came a metallic sound from beyond a plywood partition. Nerves dancing, she forced herself to take the few steps necessary to look around it.

And had to laugh at herself. It was nothing very mysterious—just a metal bucket tipped on its side, rolling over the dusty floor.

She walked down, realizing uneasily how dark it had gotten in just a few minutes. A row of the windows that would soon be put into place gleamed palely in what little light filtered in. If she didn't find Ken soon, she'd have to go back down to the car for her flashlight.

She should try him on the cell phone again. He might pick up this time, and he could guide her to his location. Why hadn't she thought of that before?

She fumbled in her shoulder bag for her phone and then stopped, freezing where she stood. She knew what the sound was now—the bucket rolling again. It shouldn't freeze to the bone. But it did.

The bucket wouldn't roll by itself; something had to make it roll. What?

Still, so still she could hear the sound of her own breath. And feel…feel the vibration in the floor. Something—

She looked up, trying to locate the source. And saw the whole row of metal-framed windows toppling toward her.

Chaos—the noise battered her, deafened her; the dust blinded her. Coughing, choking, she stumbled to her feet, staggered away from the wreckage.

She couldn't see, couldn't hear, but knew instinctively that someone was there. Someone had pushed the windows, trying to do to her what they'd tried to do to Ken with the pallet of lumber.

She gasped in a shaky breath, trying to be silent. Did he know she'd survived the attempt? Or did he think she lay, broken and dying, under the windows?

She took a soft step away from the wreckage, then another. Her head was starting to clear. The dust was starting to settle. No advantage to either of them—she could see him if he came after her, but he could see her, too.

She had to move. She couldn't just stand here and wait for him to come after her. She tried to think. The only way out she knew was the way she'd come. She moved that way a few more feet, but a sound from somewhere ahead and to her right alerted her.

He was there, between her and the stairwell. Hiding. Waiting for her to come that way—to walk into his trap.

A shiver went through her. No, he wasn't waiting. She could hear him moving stealthily toward her. She couldn't see him, but she could hear him.

Think. You can't panic. You have to think. If you run mindlessly, he'll be after you in a moment.

Please, Father, be with me now. Guide me, please. Show me the way to go.

Off to her left was a row of partitions, probably eventually intended to be exam or treatment rooms. She slipped noiselessly behind them. Darker here, but it felt safer to hide in the shadows.

Think. A plan of the hospital addition hung on the wall of Quinn's office. She must have looked at it a hundred times or more. Why didn't she remember?

She closed her eyes, trying to visualize the plan. *Please, Lord.*

Slowly the image began to come clear in her mind. The ground floor first, because it had been largest and easiest to understand. Then the projections of the upper floors. The main stairwell in the center—it couldn't be the only one.

No! Along the west wall, in the center where the elevators would go, a set of fire stairs went down to ground level.

Which way? She knew—of course she did. She knew which way the setting sun had slanted through the windows before it slipped behind the mountain.

She moved silently along the row of partitions. He was coming. She could hear his footsteps. Soft and slow, but relentless.

She moved more quickly, trying not to make a sound. Stay behind the partition, head toward the west wall. That was her best chance.

Her mind flickered back to the cell phone in her bag. It would only take moments to key in 911, but how long would it take her to explain what was happening, where she was, why she needed help?

Too long. He'd be on her long before she got all that out. Ken—she wouldn't have to explain to him, but how could she expect him to get here in time to help her? She didn't even know where he was.

No, her best bet was to keep trying to get to the fire

stairs. There was certainly every chance that she knew the building better than he did. He might not even be aware of the existence of the stairs—might think he had her trapped as long as he stayed between her and the main stairwell.

Darker now, it was harder to maintain her balance, keep from stumbling, making some noise that would alert him to where she was.

Moving slower, more cautiously, she reached what would eventually be a doorway. She paused, taking the risk of peering around it.

Her breath caught. There he was—a dark figure against a dark background. Her stomach twisted. He wasn't taking the chance that she could identify him. He wore a dark ski mask, completely covering face and hair.

She took a step back, and her luck ran out. Her foot hit a piece of pipe and sent it rattling along the floor. He spun instantly toward the sound, and a faint sliver of light struck what he had in his hand. The blade of a knife gleamed.

He started toward her. He knew where she was. No use trying to hide now—running was her only option. She bolted down the hallway she could only pray led to the stairs.

His footsteps pounded behind her. Her breath rasped in her throat. Running, running, weaving around stacks of lumber, flooring material, sawhorses—everything seemed to be stored up here, and she couldn't afford to stumble.

He stumbled. Behind her she heard a clatter as he hit something, maybe one of the sawhorses. A muttered cry, and the thud of a body hitting the floor.

It was her chance, and she took it. She ran, full tilt. Suddenly the corridor came to a dead end. She stopped, panting for breath. *Which way, which way, please, Lord—*

From the right, so faint she might be imagining it, came a slight red glow. A streak of red sky, reflected in a pane of glass? She had to risk it.

She ran to the right and there, ahead of her, she saw it. A doorway. Stairs.

She grabbed the handle, yanked it toward her, bolted through—

A cry ripped from her throat. Only her grip on the door handle saved her. Inside only a tiny landing, a concrete block wall, and a sheer drop four stories down.

She clung to the handle, heart pounding, shaking, her gaze fixed on the wall opposite her. On it, painted in stark, mocking black, was the lightning symbol.

Slowly, slowly, one shaky breath at a time, she drew back. Hardly able to dare, she turned. She didn't have the energy left to run any longer. She'd have to fight.

She stared down the dim hallway, waiting for him to appear. Nothing. Nothing but the scream of a siren and the sound of Ken's voice, calling her name.

THIRTEEN

Ken had reached the bottom of the stairwell when he heard the cry. Juli—he knew it was Juli. He raced up the stairs, heart pounding as if it would leap from his chest.

Juli— He'd known something was wrong when he picked up his messages and heard her voice, asking why he wanted to meet her here.

"Juli!" He shouted her name again, willing his feet to move faster. The cry had sounded as if it came from the top, but sounds were deceiving in an empty building. "Juli! Where are you?"

Answer me, please answer me. *Lord, show me where she is. Let me be in time.*

"Juli!" Frantic, despairing, he cried her name.

"Here." It was the thread of a call coming, as he'd thought, from the top floor.

Alive. She was alive. He didn't realize, until he heard her voice, that he'd been sure he was too late.

Thank You, Lord. Thank You.

He'd almost reached the top when she appeared,

stumbling onto the first step and then falling into his arms. He held her close, heart overflowing with thanksgiving. If he'd been too late, he'd never have forgiven himself.

"Hold it right there." The commanding voice came from below. He turned to see a uniformed officer, gun trained on him. "Step away from her."

"He's not—" Juli began, but he raised his hands and stepped back slowly.

"It's okay," he said. "I called Sam. He's on his way, but he said the uniformed officers would get here first."

"Are you all right, miss?" The patrolman had reached them now.

"I'm fine. This is Kenneth Vance. He's not the man who was chasing me." A shudder went through her, and it was all Ken could do to keep from putting his arms around her again.

The man's partner had joined them by that time—a little older, a little paunchier than his eager young colleague. "You have some ID, Mr. Vance?"

Ken nodded, pulling his wallet from his back pocket and handing it over. The older cop looked through it, comparing the military ID with Ken's face. Then he turned to his partner.

"You heard the lady. Start searching at the top. I'll take the civilians down to the street and get some help to you as soon as another black-and-white gets here."

Ken put his arm around Juli's waist as they started down. She seemed okay, but he felt a tremor run through her now and then. "Are you sure you're all right?"

"Just scared." She leaned against him. "He had a knife."

"Did you get a look at his face?" the cop asked.

She shook her head. "He had on a ski mask."

The cop shot her a skeptical look. "Seems like too much precaution for a prowler."

Juli shrugged. That was just as well. She probably realized, as he did, that there was no point in going over the whole thing until Sam got here.

"Sam will be here soon. I called him as soon as I got your message and realized something was wrong."

"Obviously you didn't leave a message at the office for me."

Her voice sounded stronger, and he murmured a silent thanksgiving. Juli was springing back, as she always seemed able to do.

"No. I didn't."

They reached the outside door just as another police car pulled up. At the officer's gesture, he led her to the car, sliding into the backseat while the police headed into the building.

"They won't find anything," Juli murmured.

"How do you know?"

She took a shuddering breath. "When I cried out, I thought it was all over. He'd find me. But then I heard you calling my name." Her fingers clutched his. "He must have heard, too. He got out right away."

"He didn't come down the main stairs. That's where I was. I'd have seen him."

"He'll have gone down the east stairs, if they're finished. He had to have an escape route planned."

"The west stairs—"

"That's where I was. That's where he chased me." Her voice choked a bit. "I went through the doorway—I thought it was my way out. But the stairs weren't finished. If I hadn't caught myself I'd have fallen all the way down."

He covered her hands with both of his. He'd like to do more, to put his arms around her and pull her close.

But he couldn't. Already a curious crowd had gathered. The police kept them a reasonable distance from the car, but they could see. A reporter and photographer had arrived from the paper, too. Anything to do with a Vance was probably considered news.

If he gave in to the urge to hold Juli, it could end up hurting her. He'd be leaving soon—he had to keep reminding himself of that. He didn't want to leave pain in his wake.

"I'm sorry. For all of it. If I could have taken your place, I would have."

"I know. I—"

Before she could finish whatever she intended to say, an unmarked car pulled up next to them. Sam got out, coming toward them quickly with his characteristic long stride. A woman who must be his partner walked off toward the uniformed officers, presumably to hear what they had to say.

Ken slid out of the car so that Sam could take his place. "About time you were getting here."

Sam shot him a sharp glance. "Take it easy, cousin. We're doing our best."

It wasn't fair to blame Sam. After all, he'd also been in on the decision to keep this whole affair unofficial.

But that was before Juli had become a target. That changed everything.

He listened as she told her story to Sam. More details were coming out this time—enough details to terrify him. If he hadn't gotten here when he did, Juli might be dead. This wasn't simply a matter of vandalism anymore. Whatever Quinn thought, they had to take this seriously.

Quinn, arriving just as Sam finished hearing Juli's story, looked shaken. "Are you sure she's all right?" He grabbed Ken's arm in a painful grip.

"Sure as I can be, but it was close. Too close."

The female officer—the one who'd come with Sam—joined them as Sam and Juli slid out of the car.

"This is my partner, Becca Hilliard." Sam gestured to them. "This is Julianna Red Feather. My cousin, Kenneth Vance, and Quinn Montgomery, whose company is building the hospital wing."

Ms. Hilliard nodded to them, apparently reserving judgment on Sam's family connection to the protagonists in this little drama. "Patrolmen think it's a simple case of vandalism. Ms. Red Feather intruded, and the perp turned ugly."

Sam shook his head before Ken could burst out with what he thought of that reasoning. He couldn't blame the woman. After all, she hadn't been privy to what had gone before.

"It's not the first problem that's come up," Sam said. "It started with vandalism, all right, but it's escalated. There have been attacks on both my cousin and Ms. Red Feather."

The woman's eyes darkened. "And there's been no formal complaint?"

"Not until an arson attempt at Julianna's home a few nights ago." Sam held up his hand. "Listen, I know what you're going to say, and you're right. I should have brought you in on it sooner."

"Yes." Her voice was crisp. "You should have."

"I'm sorry," Quinn said. "This is my fault. I've been too worried about the company to use good sense."

Sam shrugged. "Let's not start blaming each other. The thing to do now is get to the bottom of this."

But that, they all knew, wasn't going to be easy. The man, whoever he was, had covered his tracks well, leaving no evidence behind.

"We'll pick up Crale for questioning," Sam said. "Maybe we can shake something loose. Ken, you'd better drive Julianna home. I think she's had enough for one day."

"My car—" Juli began, but Sam shook his head.

"You're not driving. It's either Ken or a police car. You decide."

Juli looked too tired to argue. "Ken," she said quietly. "He can drive me."

He ought to be happy she was turning to him, but she didn't look particularly pleased about it. Truth to tell, he couldn't tell what she was thinking. Juli had put on that impassive expression of hers, and she looked determined not to let him in.

Juli's emotions were in tatters as she sat beside Ken for the ride back to her grandparents' house. If Ken didn't know by now that she loved him, he wasn't as smart as she thought he was. All she could do now was hope he didn't say anything about it.

"I should have called my grandparents. They'll be worried because I'm so late, and if they heard something on the news about the incident at the work site, they'll jump to conclusions."

"Those conclusions would be right, wouldn't they?" Ken's jaw was tight. "Don't worry about it. I called them while you were talking to Sam, just to be sure they didn't hear about it in some more unpleasant way."

"Thank you." The words were soft because there was a huge lump in her throat. Ken was a caring person—that was all it was, not a matter of caring for her in any romantic way.

"Quinn thinks you ought to take some time off work."

"I can't. I already took time off when Angel was hurt. Besides, I need this job."

He sent her a sideways glance. "Quinn has no intention of docking your pay. He thinks—we both think—that it would be safer for you."

"No." She shook her head, surprised at how strongly she felt about it.

"You'd take time off if you were called on a mission." He sounded frustrated. No doubt Quinn would, too.

"That's different. I'd go if we were deployed, because that's my duty. But I won't stay home because I'm afraid. That's letting the bad guys win."

"And you don't let the bad guys win."

"Not if I can help it. And I won't let my friends down."

There was silence in the car. Ken negotiated the turn onto her grandparents' street. Then he reached out, as if to touch her, but drew his hand back.

It wasn't a comfortable silence. It sizzled with all the things that were unsaid between them. Things like how they felt about each other.

Ken cleared his throat. "There's something I've been meaning to tell you, but I haven't had the opportunity."

"Oh?" She didn't want to look at his face, because it might be too telling, so she looked at his hands instead. They were tense on the steering wheel.

"I've been notified that I'll get a date soon for my medical exam. I'll go out to Peterson Air Base and see a doctor there."

"I see." She should have been expecting it. Clearly Ken wouldn't just go on the way he was.

His fingers tightened until his knuckles were white. "I expect to be cleared to go back to work. I don't want to let anyone down either, but when I get my orders, I'll have to leave."

She ought to say she understood, that Quinn would understand, but the words wouldn't come out. She knew what he was really saying. He was giving her fair warning that there was no place for her in his life.

Fortunately he pulled into her grandparents' driveway then, so she didn't have to say anything. Her grandmother and grandfather were out of the house the instant the car stopped. She slid out of the car and darted into their arms.

She wanted to run into the house and hide under the

covers. Or cry herself to sleep. But of course she couldn't do either of those things, because it would worry them.

Instead she had to assure them, over and over, that she was all right. Finally, with her grandmother's arm around her, they went into the house.

She expected Ken to make his escape then, but her grandfather had him by the arm, asking him questions. What did he think, what did the police think, what were they doing about this? Poor Ken didn't have many answers.

She sank down on the soft brown leather couch, curling her feet under her and pulling the woven blanket over her legs. This had been her favorite spot when she was a child, overwhelmed by life. It still felt comforting.

Her grandmother came softly back from the kitchen and handed her a steaming mug of tea. She sipped, feeling the warmth down to the pit of her stomach, soothing and unraveling her nerves.

Ken and her grandfather came in, continuing to carry on a soft-voiced conversation. Ken should look out of place in her grandparents' living room, with its adobe-colored walls, colorful braided hangings and pottery lamps, but he didn't. He seemed perfectly at ease, and when they looked at her, he and Grandfather wore identical expressions of concern.

The doorbell rang, the sound making her wince. One of the neighbors probably, coming to see what was going on. But it was Holly. She started to introduce herself to Grandfather, saw Juli and rushed to her.

"I came as soon as I heard." She knelt next to her, giving her a warm hug. "Are you sure you're okay?"

"You shouldn't have come rushing over here." Tears pricked her eyes. "I'm sure Jake would rather you didn't."

"Jake's turned into a nag since I've been pregnant. If I listened to him, I'd spend nine months in bed." She hugged Juli again. "I had to see for myself that you're okay."

"I'm fine," she said again, and then glanced up, tensing, as someone else came in the room. It was Jay, looking ill-at-ease but determined.

He hovered on the edge of the carpet. "You okay?"

She nodded.

"Someone chased her at the hospital site." Ken frowned. "She could have been…badly hurt." He'd probably intended to say killed, but changed it in deference to Grandmother's feelings. "How did you find out about it?"

Jay took a step back, as if he'd been accused. "I just know what everyone's saying. I didn't know anything."

"We know." Ken's voice softened, and he took a step toward Jay and put his arm around Jay's shoulders. "I just thought you might have heard something."

Jay shook his head. "Those guys haven't come anywhere near me lately." He grimaced. "I've been steering clear of their hangouts."

"Good," Juli said.

Jay looked from her to Ken. "I could try to find out—"

"No." Ken's arm tightened around him. "No way. We'd rather have you safe."

Jay looked up at him, and Julie's throat tightened at the look in the boy's eyes. Ken could do so much good for Jay.

But he wouldn't be here—not for Jay, and not for her.

"Are you sure this new display cabinet is going to be big enough?"

Dahlia stood in the exhibit room at the museum, her hand on Quinn Montgomery's arm. It pleased her that she could have him at her beck and call. She could feel his tension in the taut muscles under her manicured fingertips. He wanted to go, but he couldn't risk offending her.

"It's exactly the size you specified." He snapped a metal ruler closed. "As I've just demonstrated. Now if that's all you need—"

"That relieves my mind so much." As if she cared about the museum or its displays. The only thing that interested her about it was whether she might be able to take a few choice pieces with her when she left this town. "I'm sure you're eager to get back to the hospital construction site, especially after the trouble there yesterday."

He shrugged. "The news reporters made more of it than was warranted. But I am rather busy today."

"Oh, I understand completely." She kept her hand on his arm, preventing him from leaving without shaking her off, enjoying the sense of power over one of the high-and-mighty Montgomerys. "Your poor little secretary must have been frightened out of her wits."

"It would take more than that to frighten Julianna Red Feather out of her wits," he snapped. "If you'll excuse me, I really must go."

"What about the damage? There must have been damage."

"No. There wasn't." He seemed to be biting the words out.

"But there's been damage in the past. You must admit, it's worrisome for those of us who've hired your firm. I'm responsible for the museum. What if this person decided to come after us?"

"I can assure you, Ms. Sainsbury, that's not going to happen." He yanked his arm free. "I'm sure your high-tech security is up to any challenge. If you have any other questions, just leave a message at my office."

He stalked off before she could say anything else. It didn't matter.

She watched his tall figure disappear into the hallway with a slight smile. It didn't matter, because nothing Quinn Montgomery did or didn't do would change the day of reckoning that was coming to them.

She turned toward her office, the smile dimming a little. Still, Escalante would be angry that the woman had escaped without a scratch. Perhaps if she avoided the tunnels for a few hours, he'd have enough time to cool off.

Not that that seemed likely. If anything, he grew more unstable everyday. That made her challenge more exciting, balancing on the tightrope, knowing that eventually she'd bring him down. But only after she'd gotten everything she could from him.

She was a gambler by nature, just as her half brother had been. They took their chances. If she miscalculated with Escalante, she'd pay the price, but the potential payoff made it worth the risk.

At least she wouldn't have to deal with his temper for a few more hours. She slipped into her office, closing the door behind her and froze. She knew, without looking, that he was there.

He glided behind her, smooth and deadly as a rattlesnake. "You have been ignoring me, *querida*." His hands slid around her neck in a caress that could easily change into something else entirely. "Why have you not reported?"

"I have been busy. I called Quinn Montgomery over to see if I could get any further information from him about their reactions to what happened yesterday."

The grip of his hands eased slightly. "And?"

"They are frightened. All of them. Shaking in their boots about what is going to happen to them next."

That was an exaggeration, of course, but it was what he wanted to hear. His enemies must fear him. Even his allies must fear him.

"Good. They should be afraid." He let go of her, and it was all she could do not to let out of a sigh of relief when he moved toward the hidden panel that led to the tunnels.

"They don't know where you'll strike next. It terrifies them."

Let him believe that. It kept his attention focused on the enemies he knew about, instead of the one who was as close as his skin.

"Their wondering will end soon enough." His eyes glittered in a way that turned her stomach. "The Montgomerys and Vances will go to their punishment in a fiery blast, as all my enemies will die." He focused on her for a moment, and she wondered how much sanity he had left. "Remember that, *querida*. All my enemies will perish."

FOURTEEN

Ken got out of his car at the office, stretching tiredly. They'd all been working extra hours in the week since the attack on Juli at the hospital wing.

Quinn worked himself harder than anyone, determined to have the project finished without any further problems. What it was costing him in additional security and overtime, Ken couldn't even imagine.

He reached for the office door, glancing at his watch. Juli would be gone by now, and that was probably just as well. They didn't seem to have much left to say to each other.

But when he opened the door, Angel sat up with a soft woof. Juli paused for a moment in the act of pulling something from her desk drawer, as if arrested by the sight of him.

"Hi." Her voice was soft. "I didn't expect to see you here. You haven't been around the office much."

He shrugged, trying not to show that he was affected by seeing her. "Quinn's been working everyone hard down at the site. Including himself."

"It's paying off, isn't it?" She frowned, vertical creases forming between her level brows. "Surely, with the ribbon-cutting tomorrow, success is in sight."

"None too soon." He bent to ruffle Angel's ears, and the dog leaned against him, as if accepting him as a friend. "I see you're still bringing your own security force with you."

"Quinn would send me home if I showed up without her." Juli took her purse from the drawer and locked her desk.

"You're not driving yourself home, are you?" Now it was his turn to frown. "I thought your grandfather was supposed to pick you up everyday."

She shot him an annoyed look at the reminder. "He'll be here shortly. I called and told him I needed a little extra time to finish up the details for tomorrow's ceremony."

Juli had been annoyed with all of them since they'd insisted on having someone drive her to and from work, and also insisted on her keeping Angel with her the rest of the time. He could hardly blame her—Juli was an independent person who could ordinarily take care of herself. But these weren't ordinary circumstances.

"Still think we're overreacting?" he asked.

"Yes." She frowned. "But I guess I have to admit that it seems to be working. Nobody dares so much as to look cross-eyed at me with all my bodyguards."

"That's what we want." He tried to say it lightly. He didn't want her to know just how terrified for her he'd been that day at the hospital.

"I haven't been back there since," she said. It was as

if their minds worked on the same wavelength. "Is it really ready to open?"

"Near as it can be. The offices on the top floor aren't completely finished, but that won't take long. I know Quinn will be glad to see the last of this project."

She nodded, her gaze fixed gravely on his face. "And then you'll be leaving, won't you?"

"Yes." There was no point evading the question. "My physical is set up for tomorrow morning out at Peterson. By the time the ribbon-cutting is over, I should be ready to hand Quinn my resignation."

"I see." Her dark eyes gave nothing away, but somehow Ken felt the doubt that emanated from her.

His jaw tightened. "I'm *fine*. I'm going back to flying." He would. He couldn't let himself believe anything else.

And he'd been right to keep Juli at arm's length. If he passed the exam, he'd leave as soon as possible. If he didn't, he wouldn't be fit company for anyone. Either way, if they'd had a relationship, Juli would lose.

She was already hurt by his attitude, he could sense that. But it could have been a lot worse. The thought that he'd protected her was cold comfort when what he wanted to do was put his arms around her.

Angel, as if sensing tension in the air, pressed her head against Juli's knee and whined.

One thing about the dog—she made a good subject of conversation when he didn't want to talk about what he was really thinking. "Angel looks like she's back to normal after her ordeal."

Juli nodded, patting the dog. "She just needs to grow

a little fur back." She stroked the area at the base of Angel's skull where the thick fur had been shaved. "Right now she knows she looks lopsided."

"She's still a beauty." *And so is her owner.* "Jay tells me you're back to training again."

She nodded. "Where did you see Jay?"

"We've been getting together. Looking over the classes he ought to be taking, checking out extracurricular activities that will look good on his application. I don't intend to cut the kid loose just because I'm leaving. I'll stay in touch with him."

"I'm glad."

She sounded genuine, but was she thinking he could have, should have, made the same effort with her?

"Will you and Angel be headed back on active duty, too?" He couldn't easily dismiss the memory of that day she'd wept out all her pain and grief.

"I don't know." Her eyes seemed to darken. "I go over it and over it, but I still don't know if I can handle going in the field again."

"I'm sorry. I wish there was something I could say to make it better."

"I know. No one can."

She might not be able to do the job she was so good at because the pain was too great. He might sink under the pain if he couldn't go back to his. They were both still where they'd been a month ago, except that tomorrow he'd know, one way or the other, what his future held.

"Well, I'll see you at the ribbon-cutting tomorrow, at least." He tried to smile.

She shook her head. "Someone has to man the office. To tell you the truth, I'm not especially eager to go back into that building. I guess I'll have to hope I never need physical therapy."

"You'd go there if you had to. I may not know a lot about you, but I know how tough you are."

He heard the sound of tires on gravel in the parking area and turned to see Harvey Red Feather's faded pickup. His throat tightened. This was probably the last time they'd be alone together. He should say goodbye, but somehow he couldn't form the words.

Juli stood at the sound of her grandfather's truck, her throat tight with tears she was determined not to shed. This was it, then. Ken believed he was moving on with his life. Leaving was all he could think of—certainly not her.

Well, this was what he'd talked of, hoped for, all along. If she'd let herself care too much, she had no one to blame but herself.

She tried to smile and suspected it was a pitiful sight. "If we don't have a chance to talk again, I want you to know that I wish you all the best."

"Thank you. Once I'm cleared for duty, I expect to be on my way pretty quickly. It'll be good to get back to a job I know I can do."

His head was already in the clouds, she realized. If the doctors turned him down, the pain would be unimaginable. And she could do nothing about it.

However much she might want to, she couldn't fix anyone else's life. She moved toward the door, grateful that the action hid her face from him.

Father, I can't help him. I don't know what his future holds, but I know it doesn't include me. Pain gripped her heart fiercely, and she fought it back. *All I can do is release what I've felt and hoped to You, Lord. Please, protect Ken. And if it is Your will, please grant his desire to fly again.*

She was saying goodbye to her dreams, but somehow the prayer eased her pain. It would take a long time to get over Ken, but she would be all right. God would have a good, useful life for her, even if it didn't include Ken.

Words she'd first heard from her grandfather formed in her mind. Hand on the doorknob, she looked back at Ken. "There's an old Pueblo blessing that always seems a good way of saying goodbye."

She hesitated, knowing that some of the words she couldn't say to him because they came too close to the bone. But some she could say. She mustered a smile.

"This is what Grandfather would say. Hold on to what is good. Hold on to what you believe. Hold on to what you must do, even if it is a long way from here."

She didn't wait for a response. She just walked away, feeling her heart break.

Ken showed up at the ribbon-cutting ceremony because he had a job to do there, but he was essentially sleepwalking, going on automatic pilot. A small crowd had already begun to gather for the ceremony. Somehow he had to concentrate on that. Somehow he had to get through the next hour.

Then and only then would he let himself think about

what his future held. His stomach twisted into a knot as he approached the hospital wing. Hospitals. Doctors. He'd had enough of them for a while. What could they do but smash a man's dreams to pieces?

That wasn't fair, he supposed, but he wasn't in a mood to be fair. He'd thought he'd gone into that medical exam prepared for whatever the verdict might be. Now he knew he'd just been kidding himself. He hadn't been prepared at all.

Juli had known. The thought flickered through his mind. When she'd said goodbye to him at the office, he'd seen it in her eyes. She'd known he wasn't ready to deal if the answer was no.

No. No more flying, at least not jets. The damage behind his eye hadn't healed yet. Probably it never would. The Air Force wasn't about to put him in control of a million-dollar machine.

He'd been reassigned—to Peterson Air Force Base, doing training. He'd be helping other people do what he never could. Probably the powers that be thought they were doing him a favor, assigning him here, where he had friends and family.

But they weren't. It would be easier to deal with this blow away from people who cared.

He stopped at the entrance to the new physical therapy wing, nodding to the guard on duty. He'd go inside and check out the security arrangements, just as he was supposed to. He'd avoid anyone who might ask him about the results of his physical exam. And then—

And then nothing. He couldn't seem to think beyond the moment.

Anger churned through him. *Why? Why did You take away the only thing I'm good at? What is there for me now in this world?*

The blessing Juli had quoted the previous day echoed in his mind bitterly. *"Hold on to what is good. Hold on to what you believe. Hold on to what you must do even if it is a long way from here."*

He'd like to be a long way from here. He'd like to crawl into a dark cave and stay there, licking his wounds, until everyone had forgotten about him. But he couldn't. He walked forward.

"Hey, Ken." Quinn waved toward him from the reception desk in the center of the rotunda. A temporary podium had been set up nearby for the ceremony. "Did you finish your rounds yet?"

"I'm doing it now."

Fortunately Quinn was too preoccupied with the successful completion of the project to even think about where Ken had been. As for the rest of his friends and family—well, way too many of them were showing up for this event. He'd just have to keep moving and hope to avoid them as long as possible.

Colleen Montgomery, Quinn's cousin, ducked under the rope that held people away from the podium in the center of the rotunda. Catching his eye, she grinned impudently. She gestured toward the press pass that was pinned to the lapel of her cream-colored jacket.

"You wouldn't try to keep the press out of here, now would you?"

"Believe it or not, we'll be happy to have you report on the grand finale to the project." He forced a smile.

"It'll be a nice change from all those stories in the newspaper about vandalism."

"I'm looking for something more important than vandalism. Be honest with me, Ken. Do you have any thoughts about how all these problems are connected?"

"Please, Colleen." He knew why Jake was so eager to avoid her—she was too persistent. "No conspiracy theories today. Just let us get through this ceremony."

"Hey, you can't blame a reporter for trying to get a decent story." She spun around and headed for Quinn, probably hoping to get a more incendiary quote from him.

Shaking his head, he moved around the perimeter of the rotunda, alert for anyone or anything that seemed out of place. He spotted his mother, standing with Michael and Layla and deep in conversation. Judging from the desperate expression on Mike's face, the women were probably discussing the wedding again.

At least that should keep his mother from looking for him. He moved on quickly, glancing at his watch. He still had a good fifteen minutes before the hospital board members were due to arrive. He'd check to be sure the doors to the offices had been locked, then work his way back to the main door.

Everything seemed to be running smoothly. There was no reason for the harassed expression on Quinn's face, but Quinn probably wouldn't relax until this was over and he could shed the suit and get back to work.

Something ruffled the pleasant anticipation of the crowd—heads turned, conversations fell off. He swung around, nerves tightening, scanning the area. There—

by the main door—something was going on. A knot of figures seemed to struggle.

Quickly, trying not to look as if he were alarmed, he slipped through the crowd to the entrance. The guard he'd spoken to earlier was holding on to someone who struggled, trying to break free.

Ken reached around the guard's bulk to grasp the arm that flailed. The guard moved, and he got a clear view. The breath went out of him as if he'd been punched in the gut.

"Jay." He caught the boy around the shoulders, turning him so that he could get a better look at the kid's battered face. "What happened? Who did this to you?"

The guard released the grip he had on Jay's wrist. "Do you know this kid? I was trying to get him to go to the emergency room, but he wouldn't. Said he had to see you or Mr. Montgomery."

"Easy. It's okay," he said. But it wasn't okay. Someone had beaten the kid—someone with hard fists had hammered on him.

Rage pounded through Ken. He drew Jay a few steps away from the entrance, shielding him from curious glances with his body. "You need a doctor."

Jay shook his head, wincing at the movement. "No time. I had to get here—tell you what I found out." He gasped, clutching his ribs. "It's Theo. He did it."

"Did what?" He held the boy, glancing around for help.

"Somebody paid him to do it." Jay clutched his arm. "He planted a bomb. Here. You gotta get these people out. It's set to go off during the ceremony."

FIFTEEN

For an instant, Ken could only stare at the boy. Then his brain kicked into high gear, weighing, assessing. Jay could be wrong about what he'd heard. Or this could be a trick designed to disrupt the ceremony and make them look foolish.

Could be—but it wasn't a risk he was prepared to take. He met the guard's appalled gaze over Jay's head.

"You heard him. Quietly—we don't want to cause a panic. Start moving people out."

"Right." The man's voice shook.

A vivid image flashed in Ken's mind of people rushing against the doors, of innocent people hurt in the crush. "Clear the doorways as quickly and quietly as possible. The last thing we need is a panic, but the exits have to be cleared by the time we make an announcement."

The guard gulped. Then he nodded and moved quickly to the entrance, speaking to people in a low voice as he went.

"Come with me." Supporting Jay, he led him across the rotunda to Quinn.

"A bomb threat," he said softly, cutting off Quinn's startled exclamation at the sight of Jay's bloody face. "Jay says someone paid Theo Crale to set a bomb to go off during the ceremony. I've already started the guard moving people out."

"I'll call the police." Quinn's jaw went rigid, but he gave no other sign of what he must feel. He pulled his cell phone from his pocket. "You get on the loud-speaker." He nodded toward the reception desk.

"Right." Adrenaline flooded through him, and he had to force himself not to rush. He led Jay the few steps to the desk and propped him against the counter. "Hang in there, buddy. We'll get you some help soon."

His heart thudded in his ears. This was too much like those moments when his jet had gone screaming toward the earth. He'd known what to do then. And no one else's life had been at stake.

He scanned the array of connections behind the reception desk. It was just like scanning the control panel. *Don't rush. Steady. There—there was the line marked loudspeaker.*

His brother Michael loomed up on the other side of the counter. "What's going on? Can I help?"

Ken's heart clenched at the sight of him. Mom, Mike—too many people he loved could be in danger.

"No. Just get Mom and Layla out of here. Fast."

Without a word, Michael loped away. That must be a first, for Mike not to argue with his kid brother.

Ken snapped on the loudspeaker connection. By the time he'd lifted the receiver, he saw Mike ushering Mom and Layla toward the nearest exit.

He paused for a second, hand on the switch. *Please, Lord. Give me the right words. I don't want to cause a panic.*

"Ladies and gentlemen, we have to ask you to leave the building." His voice sounded smoother and calmer than he'd have believed possible. "The police are on their way to investigate a threat against the hospital. Please move in an orderly way to the nearest exit and continue away from the entrance."

For a moment, no one moved. Then the crowd began to flow toward the door. Except for one person. Colleen Montgomery darted toward them.

He repeated the announcement, forcing his voice to remain calm. No one seemed to be panicking, thank the Lord. He glared at Colleen, gesturing her toward the door. She disregarded him, of course.

"Where did the threat come from?" Colleen yanked a small recorder from her pocket, switching it on. "Was it phoned in? How reliable is the source?"

"Out." Quinn reached them in a few quick strides. He pointed, glaring at her. "Get out or I'll have someone remove you."

"You can't make me leave." She stood her ground. "Do you really want to waste time trying?"

She had a point. "Just stay out of the way." Ken turned to Quinn as a thought struck him. "The upper floors. Is anyone there?"

Quinn's face whitened. "Not supposed to be, but if so, they'll have heard the announcement. They'll start down. If they're caught in the wrong place—"

Ken swung toward Jay. "Do you have any idea where the bomb is?"

Jay pressed his hand to his head. "I heard somebody say something about it bringing the whole building down. That's all I know."

"It's hard to guess where they thought that would be." Quinn shook his head, clearly as aware as Ken that a mistake could be fatal. "My guess would be they'd try for the center of the building."

Ken nodded, flipping the speaker switch. Sometimes you just had to go with your gut reaction.

"If you are on the upper floors, please exit as quickly as possible by the east or west stairwell. Do not take the central staircase." *Please, Lord, let us be right.* "I repeat, do not take the center staircase."

He scanned the rotunda. Empty and silent. The guard waved to him from the doorway, indicating that it was all clear. He gestured for the man to go out. There was no point in keeping him here.

A siren wailed, somewhere in the distance. He glanced at his watch.

"We've still got a few minutes before the scheduled time, but there's nothing else we can do here. We'd better—"

The world ripped apart, exploding into darkness and chaos.

Juli's gaze jerked away from the computer screen as the office door flew open, hard enough to bounce against the wall. Angel snapped to her feet, letting out a warning bark.

Juli silenced her with a gesture, her eyes fixed on the security guard's face. "What is it? What's happened?"

The man sagged against the wall, panting. "It just came over the radio. There's been an explosion. At the hospital site."

It was all she could do to keep from crying out. "How bad?" She shoved her chair back.

"Bad." His face was white. "Brought down a big part of the building, sounds like."

Ken—

Her heart cried his name as her phone rang. She snatched the receiver, knowing what the call would be.

"I've just heard. Call the rest of the team. Angel and I are on the way." She hung up, trying to force herself to think calmly. No time to go home for her equipment. She had to get there. "Come, Angel."

The dog gave a short, eager bark, ears pricking alert. Angel knew what was happening. A search dog always seemed to know when it was the real thing.

She hurried to the door, grabbing the guard's arm. "I've got to get down there. Give me your keys."

Now was not the time to be stranded, waiting for a ride from Grandfather.

He nodded, tossing her a key ring. "It's the green pickup next to the gate. Take care."

Clutching the keys she bolted out the door, running across the gravel. Angel bounded by her side.

Ken. *Lord, keep him safe. Be with those in danger at this moment. Help them.*

She reached the pickup, Angel leaping into the passenger side as she held the door. She ran around, jumped in, jammed the key in the ignition.

Help us, Lord.

She pulled out of the lot, gravel spurting under the tires. Once on the main road she hit the gas, hearing the sirens wail ahead of her.

Let us be in time. Please let us be in time.

An EMT truck loomed ahead of her. She slipped behind the emergency vehicle, riding his tail, taking advantage of the siren that cleared the way in front of them.

Please. Please.

She couldn't seem to form a more coherent prayer than that. Maybe she didn't need to. God knew the desire of her heart as they roared through the city streets, her heart reaching ahead, moving faster than the truck could.

One last turn, the pickup seeming to shudder beneath her, and the hospital wing was finally in sight. Her breath caught.

Not the hospital wing as she'd last seen it. The side walls still jutted upward, red brick catching the afternoon sun. But the central section was a jumble of concrete slabs, girders, twisted metal and unidentifiable rubble.

Her heart wrenched painfully. She didn't need anyone to draw a diagram for her. A bomb had gone off right in the center of the addition, probably just when people had gathered for the ribbon-cutting.

How many had been inside? She'd seen situations like this before, but this time, the victims might well be people she knew, people she cared about.

She screeched to a halt behind the EMT vehicle. A cop started toward her, glaring, and then seemed to recognize her as she and Angel jumped out. He waved them toward a cluster of police and fire vehicles.

"Command center's over there."

She ran toward the group, her gaze searching the crowd held back by police lines. Surely she'd spot Ken's and Quinn's tall figures if they were there. She didn't. Her heart clenched painfully.

She reached the fire department liaison to the search-and-rescue team. Thank the Lord it was someone they'd worked with before, someone who knew what they could do. He swung toward her, face grim.

"How bad?" She forced the question through a painful throat.

"No confirmed fatalities yet. They had a warning—got most of the crowd out."

One of her team members tossed her a pair of coveralls, and she began pulling them on automatically. Angel pressed against her, tense with excitement.

Ken—where was Ken? "Do we know how many are still in there?"

"Not sure. One of the security guards was the last man out before it blew. He says when he came out, Quinn Montgomery was still in the rotunda, along with Ken Vance and a couple other people. They'd been directing the evacuation."

Of course they had. That's exactly what they would have done, and so they'd been right in the middle of things when the blast went off. Ken—she couldn't let herself think of him, of Quinn, of anything or anyone except the job at hand.

"Any evidence of life?" She forced the words to come out evenly as she clipped a radio to her belt.

He shook his head. "Nothing yet." He patted Angel's head. "We know what you can do. We're counting on you."

She was already orienting herself to the debris field. She had an advantage this time that she didn't have ordinarily—she'd been in the building. If the guard was right, she knew where they'd be.

Still, it always paid to conduct the search by the book. Nobody wanted to make a stupid mistake out of rushing past usual procedures.

Blueprints spread on the hood of a car, she went over the search site with her team. Four pairs of handlers and dogs, counting her and Angel, and one pair was Lisa and Queenie, who'd never done a real search. Others were on their way, but time was precious. They couldn't afford to wait.

The teams spread out, moving to their appointed zones. Lisa's hand was clutched in Queenie's fur, but she seemed steady enough. This wasn't what she'd have chosen for their first experience, but everyone had to go in for the first time. Juli gave her a reassuring thumbs-up as she signaled the teams to go to their assigned zones.

She and Angel moved forward. Suddenly the terror that she'd been holding at bay broke loose, clawing at her with sharp nails. Angel whined, pressing against her, sensing the fear. Images spun through her mind, dark images of death, of loss, of failure—

No. She wouldn't let this stop her. Ken was in there.

He wasn't dead. He couldn't die without hearing that she loved him.

Please, Father. Please. If I never do another search, I have to do this one. Please.

She pressed her eyes closed for an instant, then opened them, steadied. She signaled for Angel to begin.

With that small movement, something powerful surged through her. The link with Angel pulsed to life, as if God's hand was on them, guiding them.

Angel felt it, too. With a joyful bark she bounded forward.

Coughing, choking, Ken clawed his way to consciousness. His head was splitting, and his eyes—

Had he lost his sight entirely? He touched his face, his head, feeling rubble shift off his body as he moved.

With the movement came memory. The bomb. They'd assumed they had time to get out. They hadn't.

"Quinn!" He forced the word out, choking on it. "You here, buddy?"

The only answer was a groan, somewhere nearby. A groan. That was good, wasn't it? It meant someone was alive.

He tried to stand. His head collided with something and pain ricocheted through him. His stomach twisted. Okay. Stay on his knees. Think. He had to see. If he could see, he could help.

He fumbled in his pockets. Who else had been near him when the blast went off? Quinn. And Jay. His heart clenched. Jay was just a kid with his whole life in front of him. He'd risked that life trying to save others.

His fingers closed on his key ring with the dangling penlight Mom had put in his Christmas stocking. Silly, he'd thought then, to fill a stocking for a grown man. Now he thanked God for it.

He switched on the light. A small, feeble beam, but enough. Anything was better than being trapped in the dark. He shifted the light around, his breath catching.

It looked like the whole thing had come down around them, but the staircase, Quinn's beautiful, strong central staircase had withstood the blast enough to create a small cavern, sheltering them.

A pile of rubble shifted. Quinn groped his way into the light. "What—what happened?" He clutched his chest.

"We didn't get out before the blast." Ken crawled toward him. "You okay?"

Quinn grimaced. "Feels like a couple broken ribs, maybe. Otherwise in one piece." He moved, groaning slightly. "Who else?"

Ken swung the light around. "Jay." He scrambled toward the boy, desperately shifting debris off him, feeling for a pulse. "He's alive. Unconscious. I can't tell how badly he's hurt."

"Someone over here." Debris rustled. He heard Quinn's moan. "It's Colleen."

Quinn's cousin. Ken tried to keep his voice steady. "Is she breathing?"

Quinn bent over the motionless form. "Yes." His voice caught on a sob. "Yes. But she needs help. They both do. We have to get them out of here."

We have to get them out of here. The words rang in Ken's head. They had to. He had to. Quinn was doubling up with pain every time he moved. It was up to him to do something.

Help me. Not for myself. For them. Help me find a way to save them.

His heart winced at the thought of all the prayers he'd expended raging at God for what had happened to him. Stupid. He'd been so stupid. As if that mattered now.

Forgive me, Father. I've been so selfish. Use me now. Use me to help them. Please, use me.

"Ken?" Quinn's voice sounded weaker.

"Hold on." He swung the light around, looking for something that would tell him which way to go.

There—that surely was one of the pillars that supported the rotunda. It still stood, choked with rubble. At its base, there seemed to be a narrow opening formed by a couple of large slabs of concrete.

No way of knowing whether it would lead anywhere or not, but at least it looked like a possible way out. He set the penlight on a concrete slab.

"Do what you can for Colleen and Jay. I'm going to see if I can find a way out of here."

He crawled to the space, poking at the hole experimentally. Loose rubble shifted, but the concrete slabs seemed stable enough. He thought of Juli and Angel, searching the broken remains of buildings, pulling people to safety.

Are they looking for us now, Lord? Keep them safe, if they are.

The words Juli had said to him yesterday echoed in his mind again. *"Hold on to what is good. Hold on to what you believe. Hold on to what you must do, even if it is a long way from here."*

His heart seemed to swell. He started to dig.

SIXTEEN

Angel had a scent. She stood on a pile of rubble, barking furiously, triumphantly, her tail waving. Juli's heart leapt as she waved to the fire department team that stood waiting, ready to dig.

They scrambled toward her. Their expressions told their story—all they wanted was to do anything, including dig with their bare hands if necessary—to pull someone alive out of the rubble.

Juli's radio crackled. Lisa's voice, excited but confident and sure. "We've got something—I can hear voices."

Juli exchanged glances with the first firefighters to reach her. They'd heard, too.

Alive. They were getting someone out alive. Lisa was working the side of the building, near the stairwell that had nearly killed Juli that day. Maybe today it had been an escape hatch for someone.

Angel was digging furiously, and Juli had to pull her back physically so that the firefighters had room to dig. She held the dog, feeling the frantic beating of Angel's heart, and tendrils of hope blossomed.

Angel wanted a live find—every search dog lived for that. But she'd never acted this way before. Was it because the scent she caught was of someone she knew?

Please, Father. Please.

From the street, she heard a murmur go through the crowd. She stepped atop a slab of concrete so she could see, shielding her eyes against the bright sunlight.

They were coming out—Lisa, Queenie, the firefighters who'd assisted her—and they had victims with them. The crowd burst into applause. They were walking—three of them, dust-covered but safe.

Thank You, God. Thank You.

None of the figures was tall enough to be Quinn or Ken, but someone's prayers had been answered today.

A firefighter emerged from the hole. "Looks like a natural tunnel but too small for us. You want to let the dog see if she picks anything up inside?"

Juli jumped down, nodding. The others cleared away. Angel charged into the opening, heedless of the rough concrete that must be cutting her paws. Juli slid in behind her, switching on her light.

They were right—it did look as if the fall had created a kind of natural tunnel. Angel, whining, crept forward.

Juli touched her radio. "She thinks there's something in here. We're going a little farther."

Deeper, deeper. She couldn't let herself think of the tons of concrete poised over her. If she thought of that, she'd never go in.

The tunnel narrowed. Angel was crawling on her belly now. So was she. No one else on the team was small enough to get into this space. It had to be her.

Please, Lord.

Angel barked suddenly, the noise painful in the enclosed space.

Juli reached her, feeling the excitement that vibrated through her. "Okay, girl. Okay. Take it easy. You don't want to bring it down on us."

Rubble shifted next to her, and for a panicked moment she thought the tunnel was collapsing. And then a hand came groping through the loose concrete— a hand that clasped hers, that she'd know even in the darkest night.

Ken.

Her fingers wrapped around his, prayers of thanksgiving blossoming in her heart. "Ken. Are you all right?"

He clenched her hand warmly. "I knew it would be you. I heard the dog and knew it would be you."

"Thank God. Thank God." It was all she could say, all she could think. *Thank You, Father.*

"Yes." Ken's voice was hoarse with the dust he must be inhaling. "Thank God."

Angel, wriggling in the confined space, managed to lick their entwined fingers. Ken chuckled, the soft sound reassuring her.

"Yes, Angel, I'm glad you're here. Good girl. When we get out, I'm going to buy you the biggest steak I can find."

She forced her mind to concentrate. Get out. This wasn't over yet. She fumbled for the radio.

"Are you hurt? Is anyone with you?"

"I'm okay. Quinn's probably got some broken ribs, but he's moving around. Colleen and Jay are in here, too." His voice changed, roughened. "They're both hurt. I don't know how badly."

"Don't worry. We're going to get you out."

Please, God, we're going to get them out.

She relayed the information to the waiting rescue party, knowing that would pitch them into high gear. The problem they confronted was how to get the survivors out without causing a collapse.

"Ken, anything you can tell us about the situation will help us reach you. Can you widen this hole enough to get through?"

But even as she asked the question, she knew it was useless. Slabs of concrete lay at an angle, leaving only enough space for his hand to reach through. And the tunnel through which she'd come was too small for his broad shoulders.

"Not a chance," he said. "We're in a pocket under the central stairwell, and that seems pretty stable. If they can pull away the stuff beyond the stairwell area, I think we'll be okay."

She ought to back away so that Ken couldn't hear the conversation on the radio, but she couldn't seem to let go of his hand. Besides, this wasn't just any victim. This was Ken, a trained Air Force officer. He knew how to assess risks, and he didn't need to be coddled.

This time Steve Aigner, the liaison, came on. He listened to Ken's assessment of the situation.

"Okay, we're going to talk it over and get back to you with a plan of attack. Juli, you okay where you are?"

"Sure thing." She wouldn't leave, not as long as she could hold on to Ken's hand.

His fingers tightened on hers, as if he read her thoughts. "You ought to get out. You can't do anything more here. Just leave the radio with me."

"No chance." She tried for a lightness she didn't feel. "This thing belongs to the team. I'm not letting a civilian have it."

"Liar." He squeezed her hand again. "I want your promise that you'll get out before they start digging. Promise me, Juli."

She wouldn't have a choice, when it came to that. She'd be in the way of the rescue if she stayed. "I promise."

"Okay." He fell silent for a moment—long enough for her to wonder if he were injured and not telling her. "I wanted to tell you—when I realized we were trapped, I knew that all the things I'd been angry with God about— the accident, not flying again—they didn't matter if only God could use me to help get the others out."

She struggled to swallow the lump in her throat. "You're doing that. If you hadn't broken through, we might not have known where you were."

Until it was too late. She wouldn't say that.

His fingers rubbed hers. "I remembered that blessing you said to me yesterday. It helped."

Now she really couldn't speak. What would he think if she told him the rest of it?

The radio crackled to life. "Juli? Listen, we're all set. We'll be able to use heavy equipment to clear some of the debris now that we know where they are."

She knew what he was really saying. That with two people possibly badly injured, time was of the essence. They'd have to take the risk.

"Okay, Steve. I understand."

"Tell them to get back under the stairwell as much as possible. And you and Angel get out here now. We're not starting until you're clear. I mean it."

"Will do. Ken, you heard?"

"Right." His hand moved in hers. "Go on. You and Angel get out."

"One thing first." She pressed his fingers against her cheek. "When I told you that blessing, I didn't tell you all of it. I want to say it now."

"I'd like that." His voice was very soft.

Her heart thudded in her chest, but she managed to keep her voice steady. "Hold on to what is good. Hold on to what you believe. Hold on to what you must do, even if it is a long way from here. Hold on to life even when it is easier letting go. Hold on to my hand even when I have gone away from you." She took a breath. "I love you, Ken."

She slid backwards, leading Angel, not waiting for a response.

An eternity later she reached the surface, sliding out, lifted in the arms of the waiting crew. Angel came after her, limping a little now that her role was done. One of the firefighters picked up Angel, carrying her cradled in his arms to the waiting vet.

Juli followed, scrambling over the rocky surface. She had to get clear so that the rescue work could begin. She'd barely reached the emergency vehicles when someone grabbed her.

"Juli!" Holly's face was white. "Is it true? They're alive?"

It wasn't her job to notify victims' families, but she could hardly rob her friend of the reassurance she so desperately needed.

"I talked to Ken. They're okay." She hugged Holly. "Listen, you shouldn't be standing here. Come over here and sit down. There's nothing we can do now but wait."

"And pray." Holly nodded. Beyond the rope keeping back the spectators, Juli saw Pastor Gabriel with a group of people from the church and members of the Montgomery and Vance families, holding hands, heads bowed.

Her throat seemed to close. They'd undoubtedly been holding her in their prayers, as they would every rescue worker and victim. Sometime she'd tell them exactly how much that had meant today.

But now…now she could only watch as the heavy equipment—Quinn's heavy equipment, still present, thank the Lord—began moving the debris, bringing Ken and the others closer and closer to freedom.

"I tell you, I'm fine." Ken snatched his shirt back from the emergency room nurse who kept trying to take it. Beyond the curtain he spotted Adam Montgomery, Quinn's cousin. "Listen, Dr. Montgomery will tell you." He gestured to Adam. "Tell them to let me go."

Adam pushed the curtain aside. "It's okay," he told the nurse, smiling. "There's nothing wrong with him but bad manners."

She let go, and he shoved his arm into a sleeve, wincing a little at some bruises he hadn't known were there. "What's going on? No one will tell me anything."

Adam shrugged. "You'll have to talk to Sam for the police side. I can only tell you the medical news."

"That'll do."

"Quinn's got some painful bruised ribs, but he's otherwise okay. Colleen has a concussion, along with some assorted bruises. We're keeping her here overnight for observation, but she should be fine."

"And Jay?" His heart clenched. He'd been holding the boy in his arms when the rescuers broke through, knowing how Juli had felt when she'd held that dying child.

The anxiety must have shown in his voice, because Adam put his hand on Ken's shoulder. "Poor kid took quite a beating, between those thugs and the explosion, but he's going to be all right. He's been admitted. His father is with him now, and the rescue worker who found you—Julianna. You can go up later and see him if you want."

Juli. He slid off the table. "Later nothing. I'm going now."

"You'll have to get past all the people who want to talk to you first," Adam warned.

"I will. Thanks, Adam."

But when he reached the hallway, he saw it wasn't going to be as easy as that. He could hardly brush past his mother, or his sister or brother. And when he finally finished reassuring them and drying his mother's tears, Sam Vance and his partner were lying in wait for him.

"Listen, Sam." He stepped out of the way of an impromptu prayer service Pastor Gabriel seemed to be holding. "I can't tell you anything you don't already know. Give me a break, will you? I need to find some-one."

Sam looked as if he knew who that someone was. "Believe it or not, we don't really need you. Your friend Jay is a pretty brave kid. I'd try and get him to the police academy if his heart didn't belong to the Air Force. He's told us all about it, and we've already picked up Theo Crale."

"Has he told you yet who hired him?"

"He's denying everything at the moment, but it's early yet. We'll get him." Sam grabbed his shoulder, hard enough to make him wince. "Congratulations on not being dead yet, cousin. I think you'll find Julianna up on the second floor."

"Thanks." He saw someone carrying a camera round the corner and sprinted for the elevator, shutting the doors in the reporter's avid face.

Juli. He had to see Juli. Had to be sure she was all right.

And had he imagined it, or had he lain in the darkness with a ton of rubble over him and heard her say she loved him?

The doors swished open on the second floor. He started down the hallway, glancing at the penciled name placards on doors as he went.

Colleen Montgomery. The door swung open as he passed. He had a quick glance at a white hospital bed, a motionless figure, blond hair spilling across the pillow, a rose next to her making a bright spot of red.

He looked curiously at the tall figure striding away. What had Alessandro Donato been doing in Colleen's room?

Then he saw Juli come out of a room across the hall,

and every other thought left his mind. He reached out, as he had in the darkness, and clasped her hand.

"You're here." Stupid, but it was all he could think of to say.

"I'm here." A flush warmed her cheeks. She gestured toward the door. "Jay is in there. He insisted I bring Angel up so he could thank her, so I smuggled her in. I'm sure you want to see him."

He didn't release her hand. "I do. But I want to see you first."

The flush deepened. "You're seeing me."

A sound of laughter spilled out of one of the rooms. "Alone." He tugged at her hand, leading her down the hall until he spotted an empty room. "Here."

Once inside, he shoved the door closed. He wanted to put his arms around her, but he couldn't. Not until he knew for sure.

"Was I imagining it?"

"What?" Her face was a luminous oval in the soft glow of a bedside reading light.

"When you found us. When you told me the rest of the blessing. You said you loved me."

Her face went still. "I had to say it. Even if it embarrassed you, the way it did before. You don't have to say anything—"

He pulled her against him, his arms going around her while his heart overflowed with gratitude. "Not say anything? How could I not? I thought I'd lost you with my stupidity."

"You're not—"

He put his fingers over her lips. "Stupid. I thought

the only thing that was important in life was flying. I thought it was the only thing I'd ever be good at, and that if I couldn't do that, I was nothing."

Her eyes clouded. "The medical exam?"

"I didn't pass. I'm being assigned to Peterson, to do training."

All of a sudden that didn't sound as bad as he'd thought. He'd been a positive influence on Jay. Maybe he could be the same for a new generation of pilots.

"I'm sorry. So sorry."

He shook his head. "Don't be. I know now that God has other things for me to do. Good things." He moved his hands on her arms. "Things that I hope include you, if you can stand the idea."

Her smile came through then, trembling on the verge of tears. "Stand it? I think I've been dreaming of that since I was fifteen, and I didn't even realize it until you came back and took my heart again."

"I couldn't take what you weren't ready to give, could I?"

A tear spilled over, glistening on her cheek. "When Angel and I went in, looking for you, I knew that God had put us there for just that purpose. Whatever happens in the future, we did what He had planned for us."

He pressed his cheek against hers. "I love you, Juli. I know we've both got some things to deal with, and I'm not sure what the future holds, whether I'll stick with the Air Force or look into something else. But there's one thing I'm sure of. I love you. I want a life with you."

"That's good." Her arms went around him then. "Because I'm not letting you go."

His lips found hers then, in a kiss that held all there was of his heart.

When they finally drew an inch apart, he laid his cheek against hers. "You know, I'd like to change a little bit of that blessing you said for me."

She smiled, her cheek moving against his. "I'm not sure you ought to tamper with ancient Pueblo blessings."

"Just a little." He kissed her lightly and twined his fingers through hers. "'Hold on to life, even when it is easier letting go. Hold on to my hand, and never go away from me.'"

She looked at him gravely, and all of her courageous heart was in that look. "I will hold on. I promise. Always."

EPILOGUE

"They should be dead." He raged across the dim cavern and back again, his stride that of an angry panther balked of its prey. "Why aren't they dead?" He swung on her. "You told me they'd be dead."

She would not let him see fear. "The bomb was your idea. Apparently your experts underestimated the strength of the building. And that idiot, O'Brien, underestimated the brains of his hireling."

"O'Brien." His anger veered away from her. "The man has disappointed me once too often."

It didn't pay to relax. Keep his attention focused on O'Brien, so that he wouldn't think about her. About what she was doing, thinking, planning.

"O'Brien called me. He wants out. He's desperate, afraid Crale will name him. He wants money from you to disappear."

"It's time for him to disappear." Escalante smiled thinly. "But not in the way he imagines. Kill him. And while you're at it, frame that nosy reporter, Colleen Montgomery."

"It won't be easy. Or cheap."

"Do it," he snarled. "That should keep all of them preoccupied for the time being. Then I will reclaim what is mine."

His eyes shone like a feral cat's. Even she, who feared nothing, took a step back.

"I will reclaim what is mine," he repeated. "And my enemies will perish. All of them."

* * * * *

Dear Reader,

I'm so glad you decided to pick up this book, the fourth in the FAITH AT THE CROSSROADS series. It's been such a great experience to write this series with five such talented and dedicated authors.

As you know if you've read my earlier book, *Hero in Her Heart,* I have a great affection and respect for service dogs and their handlers. The research I did into the lives of FEMA urban search-and-rescue teams just increased my awe at what they can accomplish.

The love story of Ken and Julianna, two wounded, hurting people, put a lump in my throat as I wrote. I hope it does the same for you as you read.

I hope you'll write and let me know how you liked this story. Address your letters to me at Steeple Hill Books, 233 Broadway, Suite 1001, New York, NY 10279, and I'll be happy to send you a signed bookplate or bookmark. You can visit me on the Web at www.martaperry.com or e-mail me at marta@martaperry.com.

Blessings,

Marta Perry

QUESTIONS FOR DISCUSSION

1. In the story's opening, Kenneth Vance seems impatient with God, his family and his friends over the injury that affects his vision. Have you ever found yourself arguing with God over the things that have happened to you? Is it possible to push away the very people who want to help and support you?

2. Ken remembers Julianna Red Feather as being ashamed of her Native American heritage as a teenager, while as an adult, she exhibits pride in that heritage. Do you remember the desperate need to fit in as a teenager? Are there things you now remember with embarrassment about your efforts to be like everyone else?

3. Ken wants to return to flying so much that he can't see anything else he can do with his life, but God has some surprises in store for him. Has God ever answered your prayers in a surprising way? Can you think of examples from the Bible of times when God has acted in a way that surprised our human understanding?

4. The expansion of the hospital gives rise to opposition from residents who feel they are being displaced by it. How can a community balance the needs of the whole community versus those of a small minority? What might have been done to prevent the situation in Colorado Springs from deteriorating into vandalism?

5. Even though he tries to push them away, Kenneth has the support of his extended family and of his family's friends, people who have been close to each other for generations. Do you have a base of friends nearby that you've known for a long time? If not, what do you have to do to establish such a support group when you arrive in a new place? How can the church provide support to newcomers in its midst?

6. Julianna's work with the Urban Search and Rescue Group is very important to her, and Urban Search and Rescue has become much more visible in recent years as we've seen their work in disaster areas. What impressed you about the dedication of the volunteers who work with Julianna? Did you learn anything new about their work through this story?

7. Julianna is reluctant to introduce Ken to her family and tribe. Why do you think that is? Have you ever been exposed to misunderstanding or even ridicule because of the traditions of your family or ethnic group? How do you think you'd react if you were?

8. When someone stalks Julianna through the unfinished building, she cries out to God in fragments of prayers. Does God hear and understand those prayers that we can't fully verbalize? When might you pray that way?

9. It takes a crisis to make Ken see that some things are more important than his own vision of what his future should be. Have you ever experienced a shift in insight through a crisis or emergency? Describe how that made you feel.

10. Julianna and Ken come out of their experiences with a stronger sense of who they are and with the assurance that they have been brought together by God. Do you believe God has a hand in finding the love of your life? Why or why not? In what ways can we follow God's leading in that important decision?

*Reporter Colleen Montgomery has a nose for news—
and she smells a story brewing in Alessandro Donato.
The Italian playboy claims to be working for the
European Union, but he's been spending a lot of time
in Colorado Springs. Find out what he's up to in
Terri Reed's STRICTLY CONFIDENTIAL.*

*And now, turn the page for a sneak preview of
STIRCTLY CONFIDENTIAL, the fifth installment of
FAITH AT THE CROSSROADS.*

On sale in May 2006 from Steeple Hill Books.

Colleen studied Alessandro, liking his dark wavy hair and the aristocratic lines to his jaw. His soulful eyes could be hard and demanding yet turn so charming and compelling that her heart pounded with a rapid beat.

There was no mistaking he held an appeal that few women, except herself, of course, could resist. Like a movie star come to visit in their small community, he attracted attention.

He'd said he was an accountant. He certainly didn't come across like any number cruncher she'd ever met. Superhero, Holly had said. Determination to uncover his secrets slid into place. "What is it exactly you do for the European Union again?"

A slow smile tipped the corners of his mouth upward. "I'm gathering information to bring back to Europe on the feasibility of opening a branch of the EU Bank in Colorado Springs."

"What kind of information?" She'd heard her father and Max talking about how they'd yet to have seen any results from Alessandro's work.

"Information that will further transatlantic economic integration and enhance the flow of investments as well as trade between the EU and the US."

"That sounds like a party line to me," Colleen stated as her reporter's instincts kicked into gear. "Does such information include art?"

"Scusi?"

"I've heard from sources that you've taken an interest in the museum. And its new curator," she commented, thinking of the brunette he'd been talking to when she walked in.

She hadn't missed the way they'd stood close together, as if they were involved romantically. Perhaps that was why he'd been hanging around. Why did a bubble of disappointment lodge itself in her chest?

He arched a brow. "Really? You are checking up on me, *bella?* I'm flattered."

A heated flush flamed her cheeks. "People talk. Especially about a mysterious newcomer."

"Is that what I am to you, *bella?* Mysterious?" His dark eyes probed her as if he wanted to see deep inside her where she held her own private thoughts.

She rubbed at the sudden goose bumps prickling her arms. "I think you're a man with much to hide."

"For you, *cara mia,* I would gladly tell all my secrets."

"Yeah, right."

Not for one second did she believe him, but his smooth-as-silk tone and roguish smile still made little butterflies take flight in her stomach.

She lifted her chin. "I've heard that Italian men are dreadful flirts. You are very accomplished, indeed."

He chuckled, a deep sound that penetrated all the way to her heart. "What a delight you are, Colleen."

Unaccountably pleased by his words, she sought to bring some reality to the situation. "I doubt my brothers would agree with you," she replied as she caught sight of her two brothers standing side by side, glaring at them.

She smiled. They both shook their heads, clearly indicating they didn't approve of whom she was talking to.

Alessandro followed her gaze with his own. "Ah, the protective Montgomery brothers."

"What can I say? Do you have family besides your Aunt Lidia?" she asked, needing to turn the conversation back to him.

There was a story here. She wanted to unravel the mystery of this intriguing man, so he'd no longer hold any appeal for her. Besides, she'd promised Holly.

"What is family? Only those whose blood you share? Or those who stand by you in time of need?"

She wasn't sure how to respond to that, but she saw something flicker in his eyes, something dark and painful and she fought the urge to reach out to him. She had no experience in offering comfort to anyone, let alone to a man who was not family.

"Family can be both of those things. Family comes through connection. Whether through blood or friendship. Or through the bond of faith."

His expression softened. "Ah, *sì*. Faith. You believe deeply in God, no?"

"Yes. Very deeply."

"Because you were raised to believe."

"I was raised to believe, but that's not why I believe."

"Tell me then, why do you believe?"

"Because without faith in God there is no hope."

"So is that what keeps you going, even when you investigate the travesties of the world? When you report about an abused wife whose life has become a nightmare at the hands of the one man she should trust? When you report on the drugs and the crimes perpetuated by evil men? Is it hope that God will deliver justice? Where is the justice for the victims?"

Surprised by his passionate words, Colleen laid a hand on his arm. "God is faithful all the time," she simply said. "I don't understand God, can't fathom why the bad things in life are allowed to happen. All I can do is put my faith in the only One who does know."

Alessandro covered her hand with his. "I admire your steadfastness," he said.

His admiration was pleasing, not to mention the tender expression in his dark eyes. If she wasn't careful, she could get used to having him around.

A commotion near the entrance interrupted the moment and common sense rushed in. Colleen extracted her hand. *Having him around?* What was she thinking? Obviously she wasn't.

She didn't have time for such things. She needed to stay focused on her job.

Raised voices drew her attention. She turned to see Fire Chief Neil O'Brien push past the burly doorman.

"I've a right to be here, just as everyone else does," Neil said, his words slightly slurred.

"Not in this condition, you don't," the doorman replied and made a grab for Neil's arm. Neil dodged and continued forward, his gaze scanning the crowd, obviously looking for someone.

He looked even more haggard and worn than he had the last time Colleen had seen him at the first station when she'd confronted him about his gambling debts. His hair was mussed, his eyes bloodshot. A generous amount of weight had settled around his middle.

Colleen guessed his gambling was getting to him. She felt bad for his pregnant wife, Mary, and thankful that she wasn't here to witness the spectacle her husband was making of himself.

Neil drew up short when he met Colleen's gaze. He pointed a shaky finger at her. *"You."*

Not one ever to run from a challenge, she stepped forward. "Chief O'Brien."

"Because of you, people are saying I had something to do with the hospital fire. I told you I didn't. But you couldn't leave it alone."

"I don't for a second believe Lucia was negligent that day. My instincts tell me you're hiding something and I'm going to prove it. And if what I wrote in my article cast suspicion elsewhere, then so be it."

Colleen was aware that every person in the museum was watching, and she was even more conscious of the fact that Alessandro had come to stand behind her as if he were guarding her, protecting her.

The thought should have annoyed her. She always hated it when her brothers took that he-man stance. But having Alessandro standing watch over her made her feel secure inside.

"It didn't cast suspicion elsewhere. It cast it on me

and I have enough to deal with without your vigilante journalism destroying my life." He swayed, but jerked away from Sam's steadying hand.

"It looks to me as if you're destroying your life quite nicely all by yourself," Colleen retorted, feeling sympathetic toward his wife and unborn child. "You need some help, Chief."

"I don't need anything from you people." He turned on his heels and stormed toward the entrance.

At the archway he stopped and yelled, "You'll get yours, missy. One of these days, you'll get yours. I'll see to it." Then he banged out the door.

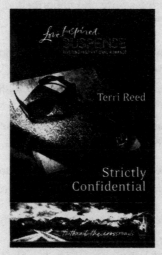

BE MY NEAT-HEART

BY

JUDY BAER

A Special
Steeple Hill Café Novel
in Love Inspired

Everything in
professional organizer
Sammi Smith's life was
perfect—except her love
life. That all changed
after she met fellow
neatnik Jared Hamilton,
who'd hired her to help
with his sister's "clutter
issues." Sometimes love
can be a messy business!

Available May 2006
wherever you buy books.

Steeple
Hill
Café

www.SteepleHill.com

LIBMN

Love Inspired™

CHILD OF MINE
BY
BONNIE K. WINN

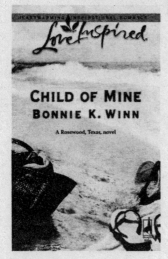

Matt Whitaker became an instant daddy to his brother's son, giving up bachelorhood without any regrets. But Matt's world was shattered when Leah Hunter, the boy's mom, came looking for the son stolen from her. Could their shared love for the child unite them forever?

Available May 2006
wherever you buy books.

Steeple
Hill®

LICOM